The Great Story of Marindel

Encountering Jesus through the Art of Storytelling

by Nathan Keys

The Great Story of Marindel: Encountering Jesus through the
Art of Storytelling
By Nathan Keys
Copyright © 2020

ISBN: 978-1-7353859-2-1

Editor: Melodie Fox
Cover Designer: Sharon Marta
Illustrator: Stacie Pitt
Graphic Artist: Michelle Keyser

Table of Contents

Praise for *The Great Story of Marindel*

When endorsing a book, I don't take this honor lightly. In the long run, it's not so much about the book but instead about the author. Nathan Keys is someone you can trust. He has brilliantly developed the first-ever, that I know of, study guide for an epic fantasy novel. Nathan is a Storyteller Champion and within his award-winning novel, The Epic of Marindel, this guide was birthed. It is an invitation to go deeper into the story, into the symbolism laced throughout the book. I wholeheartedly endorse The Great Story of Marindel Study Guide and know that it will bless everyone who reads it. Prepare your heart to go on an amazing adventure with the Holy Spirit. Are you ready?

—Brae Wyckoff, award-winning author and Director of Kingdom Writers Association www.KingdomWritersAssociation.com

Nathan Keys has produced a valuable tool that can be used by teachers and youth leaders alike. The study guide provides for both academic challenges through comprehension questions and also spiritual enrichment through reflection questions. It is a perfect tool for any homeschool program and/or middle school language arts program. Students will enjoy the great adventure found in **The Great Story of Marindel** and then will be challenged to process what they have read through the invaluable study guide. Let the adventure begin!

—Greg Letherer, Classroom Teacher for 33 years

Nathan does an incredible job of weaving powerful principles into this allegory. The rhythm with which he writes will capture your imagination and take you into deeper thinking rather naturally.

—Craig Muster, Executive Business and Life Coach

Pronunciation Guide

Auben: AH-ben

Besaadin: beh-SAH-din

Galyyr: guh-LEER

Galyyrim: guh-LEER-im

Kaya: KAI-uh

Lukúba: loo-KOO-buh

Marindel: MEHR-in-del

Marindelian: MEHR-in-DEL-ee-in

Rhema: RAY-muh

Rheman: RAY-min

Sunophsis: soo-NOFF-siss

Tethys: TETH-iss

Tethysian: teh-THEE-zhin, or teh-THISS-yin

Tyrizah: TEER-ih-zuh (second syllable almost silent)

Timeline

Time within the realm of Tyrizah is measured using the Imperial Calendar. It was set as the realm standard by the first emperor of the Tethysian Empire in the year 0 IE, the start of the Imperial Era. All years prior were labelled BIE (Before the Imperial Era), counting backward. The Imperial Era lasted for 234 years. After the fall of the Tethysian Empire, the calendar was reset to 0 AIE (After the Imperial Era), counting forward.

The Imperial Calendar is seasonal, with the spring equinox marking the first day of the year. Each year has four "months," marked by a solstice or equinox. The season and year is indicated in every chapter heading.

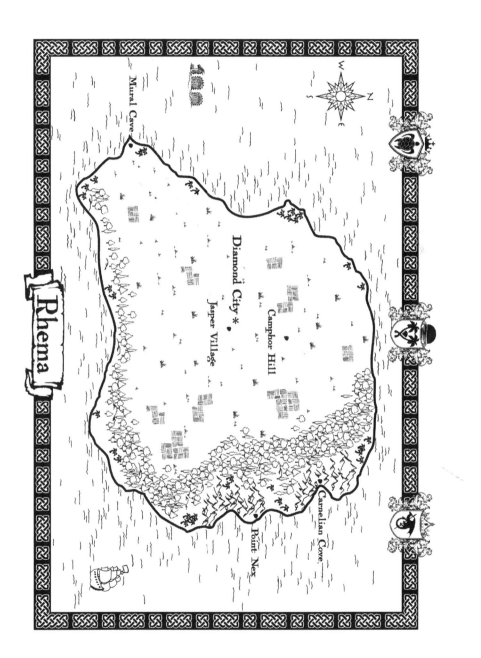

Rhema

Mural Cave

Diamond City

Jasper Village

Camphor Hill

Carnelian Cove

Point Nex

7

The Purpose of This Book

Never in my years of writing did I ever think I'd write a study book. I'm an epic fantasy author, not a teacher or a pastor! Moreover, I intentionally wrote *The Epic of Marindel: Chosen* in a way that would appeal to believers and unbelievers alike. The rest of *The Epic of Marindel* will likely follow suit.

However, I cannot ignore the demand from Christian groups and schools to include *The Epic of Marindel* in their curricula (but *Chosen* is too long to read). Nor can I deny them the opportunity to explore the many layers of symbolism in the narrative just waiting to be discovered.

Chosen's gospel allegory, called "the Great Story," was written simply in a way that can be understood and enjoyed by secular epic fantasy readers. Prior knowledge of Christianity is not required. However, the Great Story also contains many symbols and Biblical references that only readers well-versed in Scripture will be able to catch (like that pun). It's for the benefit of those readers that *The Great Story of Marindel* was written. This is an opportunity to create dialogue around the Great Story's most fascinating nuances and an opportunity for Christian readers to grow deeper in friendship with Jesus as they immerse themselves in the narrative.

The Great Story of Marindel is designed for use in group studies, classroom settings, and individual reflection. The book features fourteen chapters from *The Epic of Marindel: Chosen*, adjusted, and formatted to stand alone, with sets of questions designed to facilitate overall comprehension and personal reflection. An answer key for each chapter's Comprehension questions will be available for download on my website, www.nathankeys.com/tgsom. Reflection questions are open-ended and do not require specific answers. At the end of the book, more reflection questions and creative project ideas are available to further explore the story. Group leaders and teachers may select questions and projects to suit their curricula, or add their own, if inspired to do so.

Dear reader, this book will take you on a vivid, colorful journey to the realm of Tyrizah, where a plan for salvation is unfolding much like the one we've come to know as believers in Christ. I pray that this story will open your eyes to see the gospel of Jesus Christ with renewed, child-like faith and joy. Even now, begin asking the Holy Spirit to show you new truths about God's character, your worth in His eyes, and His astounding plan for humanity.

May you be fascinated with the wise leadership of the Great King of the Sea as Father God, our Protector and Provider.

May you be encouraged and emboldened by the passionate zeal of the Great Prince Eli as Jesus Christ, our Bridegroom and Victorious King.

May you feel seen, known, and loved as you experience redemption with Melody as the people of Israel.

Finally, always be vigilant against the deadly schemes of the Great Serpent as Satan, the accuser of the brethren.

And now, the adventure of a thousand lifetimes awaits. Clear your mind, ready your heart, and enjoy the journey!

Onward and Upward!

The Princess of the Sea
~1700 BIE

Long ago, during the Era of Peace, there was a great city unlike any other. Unmatched in splendor and power, it truly was the crown jewel of the realm. It belonged not to any kingdom, for it was never on land. It appeared here, it appeared there; no one knew where it would be next. How is that possible, you might ask? Many find it hard to believe, but this majestic city rode on the back of a giant sea turtle!

The city was called Marindel, and it was home to a thriving race of elves who lived under the governance of the Galyyrim of the Sea. Each of the Galyyrim elves possessed tremendous wisdom and magical abilities, enabling them to command the very seas they dwelled in, along with every living thing in the depths.

The sovereign ruler of Marindel, the head of the Galyyrim, and the oldest, wisest, and most powerful of them all, was called the Great King of the Sea. Together with the citizens of Marindel, he sought to ensure peace, justice, and harmony for the entire realm of Tyrizah—not only for elves and sea creatures, but for every living thing. The Era of Peace was established as the fruit of their efforts. Not a single monster or any creature of darkness was found in any kingdom of the realm at that time.

But one day, everything changed.

The Great King frequently traveled to other kingdoms to settle important political matters. A very patient man, he always traveled on foot to enjoy the fresh air and scenery. He was never in a hurry, and it was his joyful habit to stop in the villages along the way. Royal and powerful though he was, he never considered himself too lofty to spend time with the common people. He truly cared about them and sought to promote their welfare.

As the Great King was returning from an errand one fateful day, he and his entourage passed an abandoned shed on the roadside. As they drew near, they could hear a muffled infant's cry coming from within.

The Great King stopped and listened for a moment before ordering the captain of the guard, "Search the shed and bring me what you find."

"Right away, sire." The captain opened the door of the shed and disappeared inside. A moment later, he emerged holding a small baby, which he presented to the King.

The baby was human, a little girl no older than a moon. Her feeble cries and thin frame betrayed her weak and malnourished state. She was covered in dirt and had no swaddling clothes of any kind.

When the Great King took the baby and realized her terrible condition, he had compassion for her. Taking a white towel out of his bag, he wrapped her snugly in it and held her close to his chest. He rocked her slowly while gently stroking her head, and she began to calm down.

"Shall I search for the baby's parents, Your Majesty? Perhaps they are still somewhere nearby."

"No one who leaves their child in a shed has any intention of coming back for her," the Great King replied. "This little one has been abandoned for hours, or perhaps longer. She is in need of immediate care."

"Understood. Shall we press on to the next village, then?"

The Great King was silent. He smiled lovingly at the baby, who had stopped crying and was now looking up at him with curious brown eyes.

"From now on," the King whispered to her, "You will be called Melody, the daughter of the Great King of the Sea. An heir to the throne of Marindel."

Those in the King's entourage were shocked beyond words. How could the King pick up a newborn baby on the road—a human one, at that—and adopt her into the Galyyrim? A human had never stepped foot in Marindel before, let alone ruled it. They didn't understand the King's motives, so they tried to convince him to drop her off at the nearest village to be cared for by a human mother. However, the Great King insisted this girl was no ordinary human. He saw something special in her, something no one else had seen. For that reason alone, he gave her a name and adopted her into his family.

"The times are changing," the Great King said. "There will come a day when humans, elves, and sentient creatures from every kingdom in Tyrizah will live in Marindel side-by-side. I have chosen this little one to be the first."

"But what of your son, Prince Eli?" the captain asked. "Will he not succeed you as the King of Marindel?"

"He will indeed." The King's gaze was firm. "And she will rule beside him as the Princess of the Sea."

No one among the elves understood what the Great King had in mind, but they marveled at his words and returned to Marindel without any further quarrel.

Now, the Galyyrim were able to breathe underwater using their magic, but the other elves could not. Whenever the giant turtle traveled underwater, the Galyyrim created an air bubble around the city. Aside from special occasions, Marindel remained dry whether the turtle was deep beneath the sea or floating on the surface. Because of this, it wasn't hard to bring Melody into the life of the semi-aquatic kingdom.

Melody lived in the royal palace, where she grew to be an inquisitive, adventurous, and spirited girl whose beauty was noticed by all. The Galyyrim loved her and treated her as one of their own, and though the citizens of Marindel took some time to get used to the presence of a human girl in the city, they also came to love and accept her. She fit in so well that, in most cases, it was easy to forget Melody was human.

The biggest exception, however, was the physical aging difference between Melody and the elves. While the human lifespan was around eighty years, the elven lifespan was closer to two thousand, and the Galyyrim lived even longer than that. As time passed, Melody grew just like all human children do, but the elves hardly aged at all.

As part of his promise to adopt her into his family, the Great King voiced his intention to one day grant Melody the authority and inheritance of a Princess of the Sea, which included the magical powers wielded by the Galyyrim. Melody eagerly anticipated the day she would be deemed ready to receive her inheritance. The big event finally arrived when she was twelve years of age.

"Hold still, dear, I'm still fixing your hair!" A nursemaid fumbled anxiously with Melody's thick blond curls.

Melody stood in front of a mirror, vibrating with excitement. She was wearing a white dress that shimmered like sunlit marble. Her hair was tied in a neat bun with few small curls hanging down in front of her ears. She shifted her feet impatiently. "It looks fine to me. Come on, I don't want to be late!"

"Ah, there!" The nursemaid stepped back. "Look how beautiful you are."

Melody had run away before the nursemaid said, "Look." She scampered down the palace halls toward the throne room of the Great King. Marindel was underwater, so the sunlight cast deep blue rays through the vaulted windows, accompanied by the shimmering patterns of reflected water. The palace interior was dazzling on its own, but the dancing hues of blue cast by water overhead amplified its beauty beyond comparison. There was nothing else like it in any kingdom above the sea.

Melody arrived at the throne room, panting for breath. The Great King was seated on a grand central throne atop a wide flight of steps, and Prince Eli was seated at his right hand. Although Eli appeared to be the same age as Melody, he was actually much older. Despite their age difference, Melody considered Eli to be her brother and closest friend. At her arrival, the Prince smiled warmly.

Glancing around the enormous room, Melody noticed none of her other family members were present. She approached the King and said, "Here I am. I didn't miss it, did I?"

"Of course not, little one. There would be no ceremony without you."

"No one else is coming?" Melody frowned. She wanted all her friends and family to see her on her special day.

The King smiled.

Suddenly, the Galyyrim appeared in a brilliant flash all around her, dancing and blowing horns and throwing confetti. They shouted in unison, "Surprise! Hail Melody, Princess of Marindel!"

After the initial shock, Melody shrieked gleefully and joined her family in the merriment. Melody was almost as spirited a dancer as they were.

The celebration continued until the Great King stood. The company of magical elves fell silent, and Melody held her breath.

The King grinned proudly as he descended the steps toward the assembly. "Let us begin, shall we?"

Eli, beaming, followed closely behind his father.

The King said, "This is a very special day, both for my daughter, Melody, and for the Kingdom of Marindel. Never before has a human been grafted into the Galyyrim, nor has our magic been given to any creature, except through the royal bloodline. Today, both of these things will take place." At the foot of the steps, he knelt on one knee. "Melody, come to me."

Melody ran to the Great King and gave him a flying hug. "I love you, Daddy!"

"I love you too, little one." The King smiled and held Melody for a moment. He put his strong, gentle hands on her shoulders and looked into her eyes. "Are you prepared to serve Marindel to the best of your ability, no matter the cost?"

"Yes!" Melody's eyes glowed.

"Are you willing to endure the time and training required to master your magical abilities, and use them to bring forth life for the common good?"

"Yes!"

"Are you willing to take up your position within the Galyyrim with honor and respect?"

"Yes!"

"Lastly, Melody…when you come of age, will you take your place as the Princess of the Sea in marriage to my son Eli, the Prince of the Sea?"

The final question caught Melody off guard. She glanced for a second at Eli, whose excitement could be felt, but she avoided eye contact. Eli was nice, but Melody had no desire to be married to anyone yet, least of all someone she thought of as a brother. But she really wanted her powers and to become a princess, so she decided to say 'yes' and think about the consequences later.

"Yes!"

The King's face glowed with a father's pride as he reached inside his coat pocket and pulled out a plain silver amulet. "Hold this tightly and close your eyes."

Melody squealed as she took it with both hands and squeezed her eyes shut.

The Great King moved his hands around hers, close but never touching, fluid like the ocean waves. As he drew his hands apart, tendrils of silver energy swirled around Melody's hands, causing the amulet to glow. It became brighter and brighter, until a brilliant burst of blue light was emitted, and the amulet absorbed all of the silver energy strands that had been moving around it.

"Open your eyes," the Great King said, "and look at the amulet."

Melody gasped. A beautiful glowing gemstone now adorned the amulet. It must have contained every known color in the realm. "It's beautiful!"

"It was formed using your signature energy," the Great King explained. "As long as you wear the amulet, you will be able to use magic. No one can take it from you and use its power unless you surrender it to them. It's all yours."

Melody put the amulet around her neck. She expected to feel a surge of energy or an electrical sensation, but she didn't feel any different. "Now what?"

The Great King pulled out a small pot containing a dead plant. The leaves were brittle and the stem was darkened and hard. "Reach out your hand and touch the plant. Imagine you can feel energy flowing from the center of your being, down your arm, and into the plant."

Melody took a deep breath and did so. She felt a slight buzzing in her fingers as the plant returned to life from the roots up. Her eyes widened. "Daddy, look! I'm doing it!"

The Great King chuckled. "Of course, you are! Now, use your hand to guide the growth of the plant. Imagine you're sculpting clay. See in your mind how you want the plant to grow, and let it follow the flow of your hand."

Melody thought for a moment, and then she brought her hand up in a spiral. The plant regained the rest of its life and continued to grow, following the path Melody set for it. The Galyyrim whooped and cheered at the sight.

"Wow!" Melody beamed. "This is great! I *love* making plants grow. Can I do another? Please, please, please!?"

"You can beautify the halls of the palace, if you'd like," the King said. "The pots out there haven't been cared for in quite a while. One might say we were saving the task for a creative little princess like you." He gave her a wink.

"Yes! Thank you, Daddy!" Melody turned to exit the room, but the King called, "Hold on, little one. There's one more thing I'd like to ask."

"Yes?" Melody looked back at her father. She was so excited about bringing plants to life and helping them grow, that she couldn't imagine anything more wonderful.

"Since the day I brought you here, we've been unable to flood the palace like we used to. It was a necessary sacrifice, because you couldn't breathe underwater before." He paused. The twinkle in his eye said it all before he even spoke. "Now that you have the amulet, you can enjoy the flooded palace with us. What do you say?"

Melody's eyes sparkled. Eli had told her many stories about the flooded palace.

Whenever the Galyyrim wanted a change of pace in an otherwise average day, or when they desired to exercise and play with their aquatic magic, they would manipulate the air bubble around the city to exclude the palace. Water would fill every corridor, room, nook, and cranny until the whole structure was submerged. The windows would open to invite fish and other sea creatures inside, and they made for great fun—or great meals, depending on whom you asked.

Before Melody's arrival, the palace was often flooded because the Galyyrim enjoyed the feeling of unity with the ocean. Their powers were stronger and their hearts lighter as they conducted their business in the flooded palace. Melody had never experienced it for herself, but now was her chance. She responded to the King, "Yes! Oh, yes!"

"Did you hear that, everyone?" The Great King stood as he addressed the Galyyrim. "It's time to flood the palace! Let's celebrate!"

The elves cheered as they left the room. It had been twelve years since the last time the palace was flooded, so everyone was ecstatic to hear the Great King's decree that day.

Comprehension

1) List three characteristics of the Great King of the Sea, and explain how his approach to leadership might've brought about the Era of Peace.

2) Why are the elves surprised by the Great King's decision to adopt the baby?

3) During the ceremony, what is foreshadowed by Melody's hesitation to answer the Great King's final question?

4) In what form does the Great King grant Melody her royal inheritance? Under what condition is she able to use its magic?

Reflection

1)Describe the theme of adoption as it relates to your relationship with Father God. Can you see Him as a loving Father, and yourself as a celebrated son or daughter of royalty? Why or why not?

Compromise
~1700 BIE

After exiting the throne room, Melody wasn't sure where to go or what to expect. She tried to imagine the palace being flooded. Would water just appear inside? Would it trickle in slowly or come crashing through the halls? Her excitement became mixed with nervous anticipation.

"Feeling all right, Mel?" Eli's voice called behind her.

Melody whirled around, hiding her premonition with a huge smile. "Of course, I've *never* been so excited!"

"I'm sure," Eli smiled. "I'm so glad you can use magic now. How about we play a game once the palace is flooded?"

Melody's eyes glowed. She loved playing with Eli, but it would be much more fun now that she too could use magic. "Sure!"

A distant roar echoed down the hall, and the floor trembled. Melody looked out the window to see the bubble that encapsulated Marindel coming down on the towers of the palace, exposing them to the open ocean. Melody imagined torrents of water rushing down the halls, sweeping her up and throwing her around. She cringed.

"Don't be afraid," Eli said, placing a hand on her shoulder. "I know this'll be your first time underwater. Stay close and watch me. I'll show you how it's done."

The roaring of the waters intensified until, just as Melody imagined, a foaming swell came rushing down the hall toward them. At the same time, the windows opened to dump torrents of water inside. Melody shrieked and cowered behind Eli.

"Here we go!" Eli took a wide stance with one palm facing forward at the incoming flood, and another above, where a window was about to dump water. When the surge was nearly upon them, Eli moved his arms in wide, circling motions to redirect the waters and cause them to swirl around them. It was very similar, Melody noted, to how the plant had grown in the path left by her hand. As the waters in the hall rose, Eli kept the two of them dry by keeping a cylindrical wall of swirling water around them.

As the flood level neared the top of the hall and the momentum of the current slowed, Eli said, "I'm going to release the air pocket, nice and easy. We'll be in still waters before you know it. Ready?"

Melody, though still uncertain, trusted Eli and summoned as much determination as she could. "I'm ready!"

Eli stilled his hands, causing the swirling of the cylinder to stop. Then he brought his hands in close and lifted them slowly. As he did, water came from underneath to fill the cylinder. Melody stood still as the waters covered her feet first, then her knees, and then her belly.

"Don't hold your breath." Eli cracked a smile and lifted his hands the rest of the way. The remaining air in the cylinder went up and escaped with the last bits of air in the hallway. Everything was now completely submerged.

Melody, against her instinct, took a deep breath. And then another. And another. Breathing water instead of air was strange, but she was doing it. The current down the hall had slowed enough that it felt like a gentle breeze. Even so, it lifted Melody off the ground and moved her slowly.

"Well? How does it feel?" Eli asked, floating off the ground and reclining in midair—or mid-water, rather.

Melody was surprised to hear Eli's voice so clearly. Not even that—she heard him *more* clearly. She saw him clearly, too. But she didn't know how to move. "It feels funny. How do I walk? The current is taking me away."

"You don't *walk* underwater. You swim, using magic! Like this!" Eli oriented his body straight and parallel to the ground before darting down the hall. He moved incredibly fast, as if he were flying, with minimal movements from his arms or legs. On his return, he performed several corkscrews and flips before coming to a stop near a wide-eyed Melody in the same reclining position he started in. "Now, you try."

"O-okay," Melody nodded. She tried to orient herself in the position she had seen Eli swimming in, but she flailed about and went nowhere.

"You won't go far if you keep flopping around like that," Eli laughed. "You have to use magic. Focus on moving the water around you. That's what's going to propel you forward, not your own strength."

Melody nodded and took a deep breath. She held her hands forward, like when she resurrected the plant earlier. She focused on the internal energy flowing from her heart to the tips of her fingers. Then she moved her arms around experimentally. She felt the water flowing around her, following the paths set by her hands. Once she got the hang of it, she used the currents to position herself in the same way Eli had.

"Well done! You're a quick learner. Now, point your hands behind you and imagine you're releasing streams of water from your palms and feet."

Melody did so and began moving forward. A radiant smile spread across her face. "Look, I'm doing it! I'm swimming!"

"Very good! Focus on the amount of energy you're releasing to control your speed. Change the angle of your hands to guide yourself in the direction you want to go."

Melody swam back and forth down the hallway, experimenting with different turns and flips. She loved how her white dress flowed with the water around her. When she remembered her hair was still in a bun, she immediately pulled out the pins. Her hair was straight underwater, which made it appear very long. She shook her head and caused it to fan out in every direction.

Eli laughed. "Having fun, anemone-head?"

"Lots of fun!" She swam toward him, hair trailing behind like a gold ribbon, and tapped him on the head as she passed. "Tag, you're it!"

"Hey!" Eli took off after her.

Melody and Eli chased each other throughout the palace, whooping and laughing all the while. They weaved in and out of the windows and skirted the palace towers and spires like playful otters. Melody had never had this much fun playing tag before. The flooded palace was more thrilling than she could've ever imagined.

After a while, Melody entered a room decorated with large pots containing dead or dying plants. At the sight of them, she remembered what the Great King had told her about beautifying the inside of the palace. She stopped and turned. "Hey, Eli!"

Eli caught up with Melody and tapped her on the head. "You're it. What's up?"

Melody tapped him on the head. "Do plant-growing powers work underwater?"

Eli tapped Melody on the head. "Yep, they sure do."

Melody tapped Eli on the head. "But I thought plants needed air to breathe."

Eli tapped Melody on the head. "Most do, but the plants we have here can survive both on land and under the sea."

Without tapping Eli on the head, Melody said, "Oh, that's neat. Do you mind if I help a few of these plants? I really want to practice."

"Sure, go for it," Eli grinned. "Gives me plenty of time to get away!"

"Hey, wait!" Melody grabbed Eli's arm. "Let's play a different game. How about you count to, uh…a thousand while I hide, and then you have to come find me. But I'll leave a trail of beautiful plants for you to follow as hints. Sound like fun?"

"Great idea, Mel. I'll go to that corner up there and get started." He pointed at a corner by the ceiling. Of *course*, he'd choose a place he could only count in while the palace was flooded. He swam up to the corner, hid his face, and began counting. "One, two, three, four…"

Melody giggled. She gave him so long to count because she wanted to make every plant as beautiful as it could be, with time to spare to find a good hiding spot.

She approached the pot closest to her. There was a pillar nearby that looked rather bare. Nodding confidently, she extended her hand toward the plant and caused it to grow up in several vines. She made the vines weave around the pillar, like braids of hair, as thick with foliage as she could manage. Soon the entire pillar looked like a bush, but something was still missing. Melody thought for a moment, and then imagined beautiful pink flowers as she maneuvered around the pillar with her palms pointed toward it. The vines broke out with tiny pink flowers in her wake. *There*, Melody thought, admiring the pillar with a proud grin. *Now it's the most beautiful pillar I've ever seen.*

Melody moved on to the next pot, which she made into a large bush shaped like a mushroom. She even gave it big red roses to look like polka-dots. In the next pot, she made a grass-like plant that stood tall and bushy, with a single yellow hibiscus perched at the top. There wasn't a single plant Melody grew the same as another. She experimented with every idea she could think of.

As she went, Melody grew more accustomed to her powers. She had simply to imagine what she wanted, point her hands at the plant, and move them about in proper form. Soon, schools of colorful fish were drawn to her use of magic and followed her around. She enjoyed their company and pretended she was putting on a show for them. She even took ideas from her audience, creating some plants that looked like vibrant coral reefs, and others with flowers resembling various fish.

Melody had long since left the room where Eli was counting, and even forgot she was supposed to find a hiding spot. She was captivated with her task of making every plant in the palace as wonderful as it could be. She wholeheartedly enjoyed using her magic to create beauty and life.

Soon, Melody came across a pot that was different from the rest. It was dilapidated and cracked as if it hadn't been replaced in a while. Melody thought that odd since the Galyyrim put great effort into making interior design repairs when needed. Despite this, she smiled as she imagined a gorgeous flowering vine cascading over the sides of the pot to mask its imperfection.

As she approached it, the fish following her turned and swam away, but she failed to notice. Melody pointed her palms at the plant and threw her arms wide to make her image a reality.

The plant stirred with the current, but it didn't regain life.

"Huh?" Melody tilted her head. She tried again but to no avail. She leaned in closer to inspect the plant. There didn't seem to be anything different about it. Concentrating hard, she slowly extended her hands toward the plant. She could feel magic buzzing in her fingers. She lifted her hands, expecting the plant to resurrect and grow.

A leaf dislodged from the stem and sunk slowly to the ground.

Melody pouted. She pointed at the plant. "You *will* grow when I tell you to!" She tried again, but nothing happened. "What's wrong with you!? Grow, stupid plant!" She tried two more times, and then finally, with a grunt of annoyance, she sat cross-legged in mid-water and pouted some more.

Only when she stopped chastising the plant did she notice her surroundings. First, she realized the fish had left. Then, she realized where she was in the palace.

Melody had been allowed to explore the palace as freely as she wanted, with the exception of one room. Guarded by massive dark brown double-doors and sealed shut by an inconspicuous lock infused with magical energy, it was the only room in the palace the Great King declared to be off-limits. Melody didn't know what was inside, but she trusted the Great King well enough that she'd never stopped to wonder.

Now, Melody realized she was twenty feet down the hall from that very door.

It stood, looming and foreboding, at the dead-end of the hall. There were no windows or lamps nearby, so it was cast in shadow. The way the door was carved made Melody feel like it was glaring down at her.

She tore her eyes from the forbidden door and looked at the pot. Then she scanned up the hallway in the opposite direction. There were no pots in the hallway besides that one. She looked at the plant again and frowned. "If only I could make you grow. This hallway could use a little cheering up."

Do you really want to make the plant grow? a smooth voice asked in Melody's thoughts.

Melody flinched and looked around. She thought she was alone. "Hello? Eli?"

You will not see me, for I am speaking to your mind.

How are you doing that? Melody thought.

Telepathy.

Oh, nice. Can I do that too?

You may learn someday. After all, you are a much stronger magician than I am.

Thanks, but... Melody frowned at the plant. *I couldn't make this plant grow.*

Not to worry. I know how to make it grow, and if you'd like, I can show you.

Really? Melody's eyes lit up. *But…I don't know who you are.*

Yes, and neither do I know you, but I'm eager to meet one as strong and beautiful as you. Will you do me a favor?

Sure.

I've been trapped for quite some time on the other side of the door that stands to your left. I am very sad, hungry, and lonely in here. Would you please let me out?

Melody looked at the forbidden door, eyes wide. *N-no! I can't do that! The Great King has forbidden anyone from opening that door.*

Did he, now? What a cruel man he is. What is he keeping in there all to himself? Come now, you must wonder.

M-my daddy doesn't keep anything to himself. He shares with everyone. He's the most generous, kind-hearted person in the realm.

There are many things you do not know, child. Many things your daddy will not tell you.

For the first time, Melody's mind was filled with doubts about her father and curiosity as to what lay behind the forbidden door.

Tell me, why didn't the Great King give you the ability to grow this plant?

Melody frowned. *I don't know.*

He is most unfair. The Great King only gave you the powers he wanted you to have and kept many others to himself. But I know how much you really want that plant to live again.

Melody looked at the ground. She had never doubted the Great King before, and it made her queasy. Nevertheless, the voice seemed to be very wise, and a small part of her wanted to share in that wisdom.

I will give you the power to resurrect the plant, the voice said, *but first, you must help me.*

Melody remained thoughtful, wrestling with the new ideas posed by the voice in her head.

"Mel! Where are you?" Eli called, his voice distant.

You haven't much time, the voice said. *Use your magic to unlock the door. Then come inside, and I will give you the power you seek.*

Melody looked in the direction she knew Eli was coming from, and then at the forbidden door. She swallowed her fear and stilled the doubts swirling in her head. *All right. Here I come.*

She swam toward the door. In the dim light, she could just make out the lock built into the door. She placed her hand on it and willed for something to happen. Magical energy flowed out of her fingers and onto the lock, causing it to glow. It clicked and whirred as the internal pieces spun and shifted. The clamp bolting the two doors came undone with a *clunk.*

"Melody? Melody!?" Eli was close.

Hurry, inside! the voice instructed.

Without thinking, she opened one of the massive doors and

slipped inside, shutting it and hoping Eli wouldn't notice the lock was undone. The room was pitch dark; Melody couldn't see a thing. Regret came crashing over her like a wave. She sunk to the ground, curled up into a ball, and said aloud, "What in the realm of Tyrizah am I doing?"

Why are you sniveling on the floor? the voice asked. *Get up. I have another task for you.*

But it's dark, and I already opened the door for you. Isn't that enough disobedience for one day?

You are a powerful magician; there is no reason to fear the dark. Create a light and carry it in your palm.

Melody stood and held out her palm. She imagined a light appearing there, and a bright blue orb flickered to life. It floated just above her hand and even provided a bit of warmth.

Now that she could see, Melody looked around the forbidden room, squinting through the clouded, murky water. Large and circular, the walls stretched up farther than Melody's light could shine. The room was empty except for a black treasure chest in the center.

Come to the chest and open it, the voice instructed.

Melody swam cautiously toward it. There was a lock on it similar to the one that had sealed the door. She used her magic to undo it, and with bated breath, she slowly opened the chest. She expected to see some kind of treasure, like gold, jewels, or pearls. But when she peered inside, shining the light to get a better look, all she found was an elongated, twisted piece of stone. The mere sight of it filled her heart with foreboding.

Pick up the stone, the voice commanded.

Melody did as she was told. It was slimy and gross.

Focus your power into it.

Melody did so. Tiny cracks appeared, casting rays of dim yellow light. When the stone was covered in cracks, it flashed once, and the outer layer fell away in tiny flakes. What remained of the stone was mushy and limp. When it began to wriggle on its own, Melody shrieked and let go.

The thing writhed a bit more as it grew in size and adopted eel-like features. It turned to face Melody, and as it did, the voice spoke to her. *Thank you, kind one. It feels good to move around again.*

Melody grimaced. *You're...just an eel?* She had seen many eels in her twelve years of life, but she'd never seen an eel half as ugly as this one. She couldn't imagine why the Great King would go to such great lengths to hide such a pathetic creature.

Indeed, I am just an eel, it nodded. *Now that you've freed me, I will keep my promise and give you the power to bring your plant back to life.*

How are you going to do that?

Let me see your amulet, the eel replied. *Place it around my neck, and I will enchant it with the power to resurrect every plant in the realm.*

Every plant in the realm? Melody gaped. She fumbled with the amulet on her neck and pulled it over her head, careful not to let it snag on her free-floating hair. She admired the multicolored gemstone embedded within it as she placed it around the eel's neck. *It's a little big for you, isn't it?*

The eel's haughty gaze caught Melody off guard. *I wouldn't say*

34

that, dear. I'm afraid I'm a little too big for it.

Before she could question the eel's response, the light in her palm fizzled out. She opened her mouth to gasp, but she choked on water and quickly held her breath. *Wait! Why can't I breathe anymore!?*

Her answer came in the form of a flashback. The Great King said, *As long as you wear the amulet, you will be able to use magic. No one can take it from you and use its power unless you surrender it to them. It's all yours.*

Melody felt sick. She'd been tricked into giving her amulet to the eel, and now she had no powers. Though blinded by the darkness, she lunged forward to grab the amulet. *Give it back!*

It's not yours anymore, the eel chuckled. *Your foolishness is my reward!*

Panic welled up in Melody's heart as she flailed about. She couldn't hold her breath for much longer. *I'm going to drown! Help me!*

Yes, that would be unfortunate, wouldn't it? Watching you die here would be no fun at all. There are many ways we could have fun together, if I save you now.

Melody felt something touch her forehead and jolt her with electricity. She ran out of breath and inhaled deeply, expecting to choke on water, but to her relief, she was able to breathe again. She reached forward and waved her arms to find the amulet.

The eel's sinister laugh seemed to come from everywhere at once.

Melody kept searching until she hit her fingers on something solid. Surprised, she touched it again. Whatever she hit was taut and rough, like the skin of a shark. She immediately let go. *You're not an eel anymore, are you?*

Why don't you see for yourself?

Bright light flooded Melody's vision. She covered her face at first, then peered through her fingers to look. Her vision was blurry, but she could just make out a large, dark shape in front of her. She rubbed her eyes and blinked for clearer vision. When she finally saw the creature poised in front of her, she almost wished it had left her to drown instead.

It had a long, serpentine body, a dragon-like head, sharp spines like a crown around its neck, a membranous dorsal fin and tail fluke, long, sharp teeth, and even sharper green eyes. Its colors were dark blue and black with thin yellow markings, and its face was like a hideous skeletal mask. The Serpent, illuminated by a magic orb many times brighter than Melody's had been, was so massive that it nearly took up the entire room.

Melody was horrified, her face as white as a ghost. She could barely find the strength to move, let alone pull her eyes away from the monster.

What's the matter—scared? the Serpent jeered, baring his teeth in a threatening smirk. *You're not afraid of sea serpents, are you?*

Melody knew about sea serpents and had even seen a few. But in her twelve years of life, she'd never seen a sea serpent half as terrifying as this one. Summoning what little strength she had, Melody did the only thing she could think to do.

"DADDY!" She turned and tried to swim for the door, but because she no longer had magic, she flailed about uselessly.

Ha! Pathetic girl! With an amused growl, the Serpent bowed his head and clamped his jaws on Melody's hair. With a flick of his powerful neck, he threw her against the wall. *The Great King won't come to your rescue after you so blatantly disobeyed him!*

Melody gasped upon impact and sunk to the ground. She began to sob. "D-daddy…help!"

No one will save you! The Serpent faced Melody, his body moving fluidly in the tight space of the room. *But don't worry, I will take care of you. We'll have so much fun together!*

Melody couldn't resist. The Serpent picked her up by the hem of her dress and tossed her upward before swatting her with his tail fluke into the wall. With a dark chuckle, the Serpent flexed his body to pin Melody to the wall and scrape her along the stone surface. He continued to toss and abuse Melody as she accumulated open wounds, bruises, and broken bones. Portions of her hair were ripped out, and her dress was marred and torn beyond recognition. She was completely helpless. For the entirety of the beating, these thoughts passed through her mind: I did this. *It's my fault. I'm a horrible daughter.*

Before long, the Serpent stopped his cruel torture and let Melody sink to the floor like a soiled rag-doll. He purred with delight, *It's been far too long since I've had the pleasure of entertaining myself at some hapless creature's expense. Still, I cannot do much with you because you're pathetic and weak. You deserve to die.*

Melody was nearly unconscious. Pain like nothing she had ever felt crippled her body and soul. "I…deserve…to die," she mouthed silently.

Yet, I will have mercy on you, he said. *I must repay you for freeing me.*

A black cable-like tendril emerged from among the Serpent's neck spines. The tip touched her forehead, jolting her with electricity, like when she regained the ability to breathe. Her severe wounds closed up and healed, strength was restored to her body, and she could feel magic buzzing in the tips of her fingers. Yet her heart was still in great pain.

Get up, the Serpent commanded. *I have restored you.*

Melody wouldn't have moved if it weren't for the buzzing in her fingers. She didn't stop to wonder how the Serpent restored her powers without losing his own. *The monster gave my powers back. Maybe now it will let me escape.* Using magic, Melody pushed off the ground and oriented herself upright. She backed away toward the door, keeping eye contact with the beast.

The Serpent lunged toward her, jaws wide. Melody darted upward, narrowly dodging his attack. He laughed. *This will be much more exciting, now that you think you can defend yourself!*

Melody stiffened, horrified by the thought of another beating. *You said you'd repay me for freeing you. Please, let me go!*

Yes, the Serpent purred. *This room is a bit cramped for our game, isn't it? Let's go outside, you and I, to be free at last!*

Before Melody could react, the Serpent lunged and shut his jaws over Melody, trapping her in his mouth. A massive forked tongue pinned her in place. Though she struggled, she was unable to escape.

The Serpent spiraled upward along the walls of the room, gaining speed until he crashed through the ceiling like a battering ram. Shards of polished stone and roof tiles scattered about as the Serpent emerged from the tower and escaped into the open ocean. After creating some distance between himself and the city of Marindel, the Serpent spat Melody out like an unwanted piece of meat.

Melody tumbled through the water, completely helpless. When she finally slowed enough to orient herself, she was dizzy and could hardly see.

Oh, I've missed this! It feels wonderful to stretch out the open sea. Now, with the whole realm as our playground, we will have such great fun together!

When Melody regained her balance, she looked behind her to face the Serpent, but he wasn't there. Instead, she saw the massive sea turtle, patrolling the ocean depths, carrying Marindel away from her. Melody knew that if she lost sight of Marindel, it'd be nearly impossible to find her way home ever again.

"Hey! Wait!" Melody darted after the turtle. She hoped with all her might that a Galyyr would see her and signal the turtle to stop.

The Serpent's voice intruded on what little hope she had. *Why are you so desperately trying to return? You've disobeyed the Great King. He will never let you set foot in that city ever again.*

Against the pain in her heart, Melody asserted, *My daddy loves me, and so do the Galyyrim. I may get in trouble for this, but soon they'll forget all about it, and everything will be back to...*

Melody's thoughts trailed off when she saw the Serpent's massive silhouette, circling her from a distance. He had grown much larger since she last saw him. His body was as thick around as the largest tower of the palace, and he was as long as the sea turtle itself. His jaws were large enough to swallow a dozen whales all at once. With a fearful shriek, Melody channeled as much power as she could into her palms and feet as she swam after Marindel.

The Serpent laughed. *You know not who you're dealing with, little girl! Do you see how I've grown? I am the most indomitable being under the sea, stronger than any of the Galyyrim—and I will become even more powerful than this! Because you've given me your royal authority, I have the power to bring destruction upon Tyrizah, the likes of which have never been seen. Surely you have placed a death sentence on your own head and on every living thing in the realm. Not even the Great King will forgive you for such a crime. He will surely hate you!*

The Serpent's accusation crippled Melody's soul so badly that she lost the will to pursue Marindel. She watched as the turtle-borne city grew smaller and smaller before fading away into the ocean blue.

As Marindel disappeared, the Serpent said, *They will all hate you. Not just them, but those above as well. No one will welcome you into their city. They will chase you and try to kill you for no reason at all, except for pure hatred. You will live out the years of the long life the Great King has given you in great misery.*

Melody closed her eyes. *It's all my fault. I'm so naive, so stupid and worthless. No one will ever love a horrible person like me. You're right, I can't return to Marindel. My father will disown me. I deserve to die!* The last thought caused her to sob.

Finally, you have come to your senses. You're nothing but a runaway and a criminal. Begone from the sea, and embrace the suffering you've brought upon yourself.

Melody didn't resist as the Serpent came near and coiled a black tendril around her. He carried her up to the surface of the deep and leapt into the air. At the pinnacle of his flight, the Serpent hurled Melody with all his might, sending her tumbling over the horizon and out of sight. With a victorious roar, the Serpent plummeted back into the ocean and disappeared into the darkness.

Eli opened the forbidden door and stood at the entrance. He'd felt the palace tremble when the Serpent escaped, and he desperately hoped Melody wasn't the cause of it. "Mel!? Melody, where are you!?"

The Great King entered, passing Eli to stop at the center of the room, where he saw the black chest broken into pieces. The water was tainted with blood, and bits of Melody's dress and hair were scattered along the floor. A ray of light from the gaping hole in the ceiling illuminated the pitiful sight.

The King fell to his knees and wept. "Oh, no! Melody, my beautiful daughter! This can't be!"

Eli frowned as he approached. "Father? What happened? Is Melody...?"

The Great King, consumed with anguish, could say nothing but his beloved child's name.

Eli had never seen his father so distraught. Fearing the worst, he began to weep as well. The two of them wept until they were spent, unable to say a word.

Hours later, the Great King mustered his strength and said, "My son, you must understand—Melody has done a very terrible thing by surrendering her inheritance to the Great Serpent."

Eli looked up at the King with wide eyes.

"Tyrizah will not be the same. It will be filled with chaos, perversion, destruction, and death. There is no easy solution, for as long as the Serpent has Melody's inheritance, none of us can stop him. Moreover, only she can reclaim what is rightfully hers."

"Will she?" Eli asked.

"No," the Great King's eyes welled up. "Not without help."

Eli picked up a blood-stained fragment of Melody's dress. He was flooded with memories of playing with her when she was little. He taught her about life in Marindel and showed her around the city. He was with her when she learned to play the piano, and they even created songs together. They would often play tag in the palace halls and gardens, though Eli never used his powers and almost always let her win. He remembered how his heart burned with excitement when the Great King told him they would be married if she agreed to it. But that could never happen now. Unless…

"I will help her!" Eli declared. He stood and looked at the King, a zealous fire kindling in his gaze. "Send me, Father! I'll do whatever it takes to save Melody and help her reclaim her inheritance."

The Great King looked at his son with mixed compassion and determination. "Very well, my son. When the time is right, I will send you to the realm above to find her. In the meantime, prepare yourself and wait patiently."

Comprehension

1) List three adjectives that describe Eli and Melody's relationship.

2) For what reason does Melody suggest playing hide-and-seek?

3) How does the voice disrupt Melody's trust in the Great King?

4) Why do you think the Serpent gives Melody her powers back?

5) Why can't the Kingdom of Marindel directly stop the Great Serpent?

Reflection

1) If you had the power to create any plant or tree, what would it be, and why? Feel free to draw your answer.

2) While it's sometimes good to investigate and question our own beliefs so that we learn and grow, how can we ensure we don't lose sight of the ultimate Truth of God's Goodness?

3

The Kingdom of Rhema
~1700 BIE — 104 IE

Everything the Great King said would happen came to pass. With the power granted by Melody's inheritance, the Great Serpent was unstoppable, and he asserted control over every living thing in the realm. Wars broke out, natural disasters and horrible monsters ravaged the land, and diseases spread unabated. The Era of Peace came to a swift end, and in its place came a terrible era of darkness and despair.

Unfortunately, not even the Kingdom of Marindel was safe. Soon after his release, the Serpent mobilized an army of powerful monsters and hideous creatures from the Bygone Era, and he led them in a direct assault against the Great King and the Galyyrim to destroy the Kingdom of Marindel once and for all.

The Great King, wise and sovereign in his leadership, knew the Serpent could not be stripped of his power through outright confrontation. He also knew that the Kingdom of Marindel could not safely exist in a realm subdued by the Serpent. To save what he could of the city and those loyal to him, he ordered the Royal Orchestra to play the Music of Marindel, of which it is said,

"The Music of Marindel,
A song devoted to the Great King,
Will turn the tide of battle,
Banish the curse from land afflicting,
Pacify the ruthless beast,
And strengthen hearts of those found trembling."

The song of thousands of voices and instruments, playing in perfect harmony unto the King, repelled the Serpent's dark forces and caused the Kingdom of Marindel to vanish from the realm of Tyrizah. No living creature has seen it since.

For many centuries, it seemed as though the Serpent reigned unchallenged. Marindel was gone, the Great King was nowhere to be found, and every creature on land and under the sea was subject to the Serpent's heartless cruelty with no hope for a better future. However, the Great King hadn't forgotten about the realm he loved so fiercely, and he had a plan to rescue it from the Serpent's grasp.

Melody, the King's lost daughter, had been hurled by the Serpent into the realm above the sea. Every day, for many years, she was chased around and mistreated for no reason at all, except for pure hatred. The lies the Serpent spoke to her on the day of his release were driven deep into her soul. She believed she was despised by the Great King and could never return to Marindel, even if she wanted to. As a result, she lived her life independently and full of misery, knowing she deserved to die for all the darkness she unleashed upon the realm.

In time, the Great King began whispering to her. His gentle voice in her heart began melting the callousness caused by the Serpent's lies and others' harsh treatment of her. She began to realize there was something she was made for, some sort of purpose, but she couldn't discern what it was. The Serpent kept her blind to it.

When Melody had the appearance of fourteen years of age,

around the year 1200 BIE, she obeyed a prompt from the Great King to travel to a new land. As she journeyed across the mainland, many people joined her on her quest. The Serpent retaliated by sending enemy armies and bloodthirsty monsters to dispel the group, but the Great King protected them from every attack as they followed his lead.

From the southern shore of the mainland, Melody and two hundred adventurers set sail into unknown waters. Following directions from the Great King, they happened upon a pristine island paradise in the middle of the sea. There they settled and built towns, villages, and cities. Melody named the island Rhema, in honor of the gentle whispers of the King who led her there.

In the early years, Rhema was the most peaceful land in the realm. Though little was known or understood about the Great King at that time, everyone on the island acknowledged him. Many years passed, and the people of Rhema multiplied and prospered.

Unfortunately, so too did the seed of pride in Melody's heart.

She wanted so badly to believe she was important and self-reliant, but with the lies of the Serpent so deeply rooted in her soul, she couldn't cure her sense of guilt and worthlessness. The Serpent took advantage of Melody's thoughts and slowly convinced her that she'd built Rhema all on her own, and she deserved to be its rightful queen.

When she had the appearance of sixteen years of age, without giving any thought to the will of the Great King, Melody asserted herself as the Queen of Rhema and declared it to be an official kingdom. This happened in the year 618 BIE. From then on, though they maintained the appearance of prosperity, Melody and her people forgot about the Great King. They became entangled in the affairs of other kingdoms across the sea. Alliances were made, battles were fought, and worst of all, the Serpent's corruption saturated the hearts and minds of the citizens of Rhema. Melody and her appointed officials, poisoned with arrogance, ignored the plight of the poor and denied justice to the innocent. They even encouraged other kingdoms to do the same.

During that time of slow decline, several Rhemans remembered the Great King and everything he did for them. These individuals were empowered to be the first Seers—people who could discern hidden details about past, present, and future events. Over a period of several hundred years, they warned Melody that if she and her people didn't follow the ways of the Great King as they had done before, Rhema would be subject to an onslaught of the Serpent's cruelty.

Melody never listened to the Seers. She came to despise them for meddling in her affairs and never having anything good to say. In time, she ordered them to be exiled or killed as enemies of the kingdom.

The final Seer of those days, before his execution, pleaded with Melody, "Your father, the King, remembers you, and he loves you! The Prince of the Sea is coming soon, and he will deliver you from the power of the Serpent once and for all! Remember the Great King and follow his ways! He doesn't want you to continue in your suffering, but to return to Marindel as the bride of the Great Prince."

"Kill him," Melody said, and the deed was done.

Two centuries later, when Melody had the appearance of nineteen years of age, the kingdoms of Tyrizah were terrorized by the rapid expansion of the Tethysian Empire, notorious for their use of dragons in military combat. Most kingdoms hadn't the means to resist such a novel strategy.

As the Empire's expansion brought war closer and closer to Rhema, Melody and her officials were terrified. To avoid an attack they feared was imminent, in 57 IE, they sent ambassadors to the emperor to form a compromise. The terms of the treaty allowed the Empire to occupy Rhema and use it as a launch point into the southern mainland kingdoms, while sparing the citizens of Rhema and allowing Melody's regime to remain in power, albeit under the higher command of the emperor.

During this dark period of history, the stage was set for the next phase of the Great King's plan:

The adventure of a thousand lifetimes.
The most incredible romance ever recounted.
The greatest battle of all time.
The beginning of the Return of Marindel.

On the appointed day, the Great King said to Prince Eli, "My son, the time has come. Melody is of age, and the kingdoms of the realm are aligned according to plan."

"I'm ready, Father," Eli replied.

"Before you go, you must understand—Melody's heart is harder now than ever before. She's not the same little girl you played with in the palace gardens during the Era of Peace. She will not recognize you, nor will she want to. You must surrender your powers and your Marindelian heritage to become just like her in every way. Lower yourself to love her and bring her heart out of the slimy pit in which the Serpent has buried it. Show her what it means to care deeply for the welfare of her people. Though you will have no power of your own, I will be your guide and your source of strength. In this way, you will set an example not only for Melody, but for all sentient creatures in every kingdom of Tyrizah for years to come. Do you understand?"

"Yes, Father. I'll do whatever it takes."

The Great King's voice quivered with emotion. "Remember, I will never abandon you, and my love is always with you. Go now! Tell my daughter everything that is stored up in your heart."

Comprehension

1)How does the Great King save Marindel from the Great Serpent's attack?

2)Define the Greek word "rhema." Why does Melody name the island Rhema?

3)Which of Melody's weaknesses does the Serpent exploit to corrupt Rheman society? What is the end result?

4)What must Eli do to be successful in his mission to rescue Melody?

Reflection

1)Read Psalm 18:3-6, 16-19. Can you recall a time when God led you into a "spacious place?" Describe the challenges you faced and how He answered your plight.

The Prince of the Sea
Summer, 104 IE

Over the vast expanse of the sea, from a place no one could fathom, came a small sailboat driven by a southbound wind. Entering the harbor sheltered on either side by tall wooded hills, not a single alarm did sound. Laying anchor at the busy docks of Carnelian Cove, no one so much as lifted their head.

A young man stepped off the boat, clothed in nothing more than a brown commoner's tunic. His raven-black hair, sprinkled with sea salt, shone in the sun. His stature was strong and stately, yet gentle. In his amber eyes was a fiery hope that could not be quenched.

He looked out at the sailors, farmers, merchants, craftsmen, and soldiers who went about their business on this ordinary day in the kingdom of Rhema.

Not a single person acknowledged him.

Indeed, for the first time in this man's life, not a single knee bowed.

He spared no time, for he knew exactly what he had come to do. Approaching a pair of sailors, he greeted them, "Good afternoon, gentlemen. Do you know where Melody is today?"

"Ah, lucky for you, she happens to be in town. I think she'll be having an important meeting with the Tethysians."

The other sailor narrowed his eyes. "Why do you ask, stranger? You aren't hoping to meet her, are you? She's not the friendly type. Doesn't take well to commoners, they say."

"That's not the Melody I know," the man replied. "She has forgotten who she is and the family to whom she belongs. But I will help her see."

"What are you talking about?" the second sailor scoffed. "She knows full well who she is: the Queen of Rhema, head of the aristocratic snobs, and a pawn of the Tethysian Empire. You're wasting your time! Go back to wherever it is you're from."

"I will not go until I fulfill my mission," the man replied. "I will not leave her a victim of darkness any longer. It's time for Melody to remember where she belongs as true royalty."

The sailors laughed at him.

"Go on, then!" the first sailor said. "Make a fool of yourself before the officials of Rhema and the Empire!"

With a parting nod, the man left the sailors and went into town.

Melody stepped out onto the front balcony of the town hall. With an exasperated sigh, she leaned against the stone banister and looked out at the city. She could see all of Carnelian Cove from there because the town hall was built on higher ground at the back of the cove.

Two of Melody's appointed officials, elders in the royal court, came out shortly after her.

"What hope is there?" Melody asked, as they stood on either side of her. "I'm losing my kingdom and everything I've worked so hard to build."

"Milady, don't be worried," said one of the elders, whose beard was angular and silky-white. "For the good of Rhema, we *must* cooperate with the Tethysians. They're stronger than we are, but with their protection, we can rest content beneath their wings."

Melody sighed again. "I know, but I *hate* it. I wish I could change the way things are."

"There may be nothing you can do," the white-bearded elder said. "But no matter what comes, we will always stand with you as your advisers and friends. We live and breathe to serve you and the people of Rhema according to the royal traditions of this great kingdom."

The other elder, having a big nose, spoke next. "Milady, you know better than anyone how far we've come as a kingdom. How many trials have we overcome through your vast resources and intelligent strategies? Don't be worried! Even this will soon come to—"

"Look," Melody interrupted, pointing over the side of the banister. "Who's that?"

The three looked down at the cobblestone road to see a man approaching them.

"Hmph. Just a commoner," the big-nosed elder said.

"What business does a commoner have at the town hall?" Melody asked.

"None whatsoever," the white-bearded elder said, leering down at the man.

The newcomer waved and called, "Melody! How great it is to see you!"

"What do you want?" Melody called back.

"You may not remember me," the man said, standing below the balcony, "but I'm an old friend. Come and see for yourself!"

"I'm not going *down there*," Melody said, curling her lip.

"Leave the queen alone," the big-nosed elder called.

"Wait a moment, just hear me out," the man said, his face beaming. "My name is Eli, and I've come from the Kingdom of Marindel."

Several emotions flashed across Melody's face, but she suppressed them at once. Lifting her chin, she said, "I don't know who you are. Go away."

"I can help you remember."

The white-bearded elder said, "How dare you oppose a direct order from your queen! We know everything there is to know about Marindel, and you are most certainly *not* from there. Begone with you!"

Eli ignored the elder. "Melody, please. If you only knew how much my heart has yearned for this day—the day the Great King has sent me to find you! I'm Prince Eli, your friend! Come walk with me, and I'll show you."

"No! Go away!"

A small part of Melody's soul did remember Eli, but she didn't want to believe he was the one addressing her now. To her, Eli was only a distant memory that died when the Serpent claimed her mind and her heart.

Eli, though visibly saddened, nodded in concession. "All right. But Melody, I want you to know that I love you, and I'm not giving up on you. My father and I will never give up on you."

"Ugh!" Melody turned and stormed back into the town hall.

The white-bearded elder glared down at Eli. "Look, now you've done it! Begone with you, and never show your face around here again!"

Eli replied, "You think you're Melody's greatest protectors and her sole source of guidance, but in reality, you are the Serpent's blind puppets. You're leading her and the whole kingdom of Rhema to its destruction."

At that, Eli turned and walked away, back down the hill.

The elders were shocked. They exchanged glances, and the white-bearded elder asked, "Did you just hear that?"

"Poppycock," the big-nosed elder scoffed.

"Blind puppets, indeed! Have you ever seen a man more drunk than he?"

"Not one."

"Hmph. Well, at least we know we won't be seeing *him* again. No self-appointed suitor from any kingdom, honest or drunk, would dare pursue Melody after a rejection like that."

The two elders chuckled as they turned and vanished into the town hall.

After that encounter, Eli left Carnelian Cove and began traveling on foot to Diamond City, the capital of Rhema. Around midnight, as he was walking through the woods, the Serpent spoke to him.

Well, if it isn't the Great Prince himself, come to grace my realm with his glamorous presence.

Eli ignored the Serpent and continued onward.

What are you trying to prove? the Serpent pressed. *You left your cozy palace, your whole family, and all your powers behind, just to be rejected again and again by a worthless human girl.*

"The Great King's plans are far greater than you can imagine," Eli said.

Oh no, if I were you, I would watch my tongue. You're on my turf now. Melody is mine, Rhema is mine, the whole realm answers to me. You ought to give up now while you have a chance. Acknowledge your defeat and bow to me.

"I answer only to my father, the Great King. Your ownership of this realm is only a shadow. Even *you* know that shadows must flee when the light comes."

Ha! You couldn't defeat me even if you came with all of your power, and all of the Galyyrim by your side. How do you, a mere man, expect to challenge me?

Eli ignored the Serpent and continued onward.

Tell me, Prince, the Serpent hissed as supernatural darkness fell upon the woods. *Why did your daddy really send you here? Don't bother defending him; you know it's true. He disowned you and sent you away. There's no other explanation. You see, the girl* willingly *surrendered her authority to me. I am in power now, forever, and for all time. She traded her inheritance for a death sentence. A slow, painful, all-consuming death. That is her inheritance now, forever, and for all time. And it can never be undone.*

Eli stood still.

As the Serpent continued, dark forms moved about in the shadows, and the sound of rustling insect wings could be heard. *Face it, my noble adversary. There is no path forward for you here. The Great King knows better than anyone that the human girl cannot be saved. Can't you see? He sent you here to die. Come now, give up and go home. Why must you give yourself to such a miserable fate?*

"Be quiet!" Eli's rebuke sent a tremor through the darkness. "I've come willingly to this land, following the guidance of my father the King, to take Melody's inheritance upon myself. *I* will take the punishment for the wrongdoing she has unleashed upon herself and the realm."

Hmph. Hmhmhm... Hahahaha! You really are a fool! I must say, I expected better from you. But how can I refuse? The Great King has chosen to save his human pet by slaying his blood-born son, the heir to the throne of Marindel. Ha! Hahahaha!

The shadows, creeping closer, laughed in chorus with the Serpent.

Eli clenched his fists. "Are you finished yet?"

I'm afraid not, oh mighty Prince. I'm only getting started. A thin tendril of darkness caressed Eli's cheek. *I will take you up on your offer. But, lest you convince yourself you're doing something noble, allow me to let you in on a little secret: I will make it hurt. I will inflict upon you excruciating pain unlike anything you've ever imagined. And what's more, I will rip your father's heart out of his chest and shred it to ribbons with the way I will dispose of you. I'll destroy everything the Great King loves most, beginning with you.*

"That's enough! Begone!"

The darkness recoiled and disappeared.

Alone in the woods once again, with the stars casting faint dappled light through the canopy, Eli said, "Father, I trust you."
And he continued on to Diamond City.

Along the way, Eli made frequent stops in the towns and villages along the road. He spent time with the common people, told them stories of the Kingdom of Marindel, helped those who were in need, and spoke out against injustices committed by Melody's officials, who often sought to challenge him. Eli did these things, cherishing the people in every village he passed, just like his father, the Great King, did long ago.

Two weeks later, Melody was walking through the Diamond City marketplace with a few of her officials in tow. As she browsed the various fruit stands where farmers displayed their seasonal goods, she grumbled to herself, "No one knows how to grow high-quality fruit anymore. It's all mushy, spotted, and rotten, and it costs *twice* as much as it's worth! What has become of this kingdom?"

One of her officials was close enough to hear the complaint. He said, "Milady, you could pass a law about that; a decree for the price of fruit to be dropped to what it's worth, or a command to simply grow better fruit. You know, most farmers probably keep the good fruit to themselves, and they only sell what they don't want. How selfish of them, wouldn't you say?"

"Very much so," Melody agreed, glaring at the farmers who sat behind the fruit stands. Her eyes locked onto a man selling pineapples, and she went toward him.

When she came near, the farmer looked up and gasped. "Oh, Milady! What a pleasant surprise! Please, have a look at my—"

"Rubbish, peasant! I *did* have a look at your foul-smelling crop, and I hated every second of it! What's the matter with you!?"

Melody's words hit the farmer, like a mallet on a tent peg, until only the top of his terrified face was visible behind the stand. "I-I don't understand why you're not pleased, Milady…"

Melody picked up a pineapple and pointed at a blemish. "What is this!?"

"It's, uh…it's a unicorn hoof-print."

"A unicorn hoof-print!" Melody spat. "What in the kingdom of Rhema was a unicorn doing stepping on your pineapples!?"

"They live in the fields around here, surely you know! They aren't careful as they—"

"You idiot! Build a fence! Get a dog! Do *something*! How do you expect anyone to buy this garbage!?"

"I-I, uh…" The farmer, his face beet-red with embarrassment, sought words in vain.

The officials stood behind Melody, pointing and laughing at the farmer's humiliation.

Melody continued, "Why don't you do the whole kingdom a favor and cut the price? How about you sell them for one kappe each? Then, maybe a starving child would buy it—to throw at his brother and knock him out to claim the last grain of rice!"

"Milady, I'm so sorry! I'll do whatever you'd like, just *please* have mercy!"

Melody scoffed. "Mercy? I'll show you mercy!"

She raised the pineapple, ready to smash it over the farmer's head.

"Melody!" a voice called.

Her arm stopped as if someone had grabbed it.

Everyone standing within a twenty-foot radius of the spectacle went quiet.

The officials exchanged bewildered glances. Melody looked at them, wondering which of them had called her, but they shrugged and shook their heads.

The crowd adjacent to the officials parted and Eli stepped forward. His voice was fraught with sadness as he spoke. "Melody, what are you doing?"

She recognized him from Carnelian Cove. She hadn't been able to shake the thought of him since that encounter, and seeing him now caused her heart to drop. She tensed and glared at him. "Why do *you* care?"

Eli stood alongside the officials. "I care deeply when my father's people are abused by the one he chose to protect them."

"Hmph. What are you talking about?"

"Why were you about to hit that innocent man in the face with a pineapple?"

Melody was caught off guard by his frankness. She held up the fruit and pointed at the blemish. "Look. He let a unicorn step all over his field, and this is what happened. Now he expects everyone to pay an outrageous price for his mistake. He's far from innocent and deserves a beating for his conniving, selfish attitude!"

"I don't see a blemish," Eli said.

"Well, you're blind then," Melody sneered. "It's big and obvious, right—" she gasped.

The blemish was gone.

People in the crowd gasped and muttered amongst themselves.

The pineapple farmer rose out of hiding to see what was happening.

Eli kept his gaze on Melody. "You were saying?"

"Huh?" Melody turned the pineapple around and around, searching for the missing blemish to no avail. "It was just here! I saw it! You all saw it, right?" She looked to her officials.

They stood by without a word. They were as stunned as she was.

"Wow!" a woman in the crowd said. "Those pineapples look delicious!"

Everyone looked at the pineapple stand, which was now filled with the most delectable pineapples that ever graced the kingdom of Rhema.

The farmer's jaw dropped wide open as he beheld his crop.

Melody couldn't believe her eyes. She turned on Eli and asked, "What did you just do!?"

"My father is pleased to bless a simple man, as well as to set an example of mercy for those to whom he has given authority."

The crowd began surging toward the pineapple stand to buy the delicious fruit. The officials stood in the way, shouting, "Don't buy from this man! His crop is cursed! You saw what happened with your own eyes! Where's your common sense?" But the people barged past them, waving handfuls of coins in the air and shouting over one another to barter for the fruit. The officials were so caught up in trying to dissuade the crowd, they didn't notice Melody and Eli conversing nearby.

Melody stepped up close to Eli and glared at him. "Who do you think you are? And who is this father of yours?"

Eli met her gaze firmly. "I've already told you, but you didn't listen. I'm Prince Eli of Marindel, and my father is the Great King."

"You're crazy! Get out of here!"

"Melody, you know it's true. I see it in your eyes. Please, let go of your unbelief and trust me."

Melody trembled at his words. This peasant's persistence was frightening. When she could finally mouth a reply, she said, "You don't know me, and you don't know Eli. You're a monster sent to destroy me!"

"No." Eli put his hand on Melody's quaking shoulder. Their

faces were inches apart now, and the chaotic marketplace faded into the background. "I know you, Melody. I've known you since the day you were brought into Marindel, the city on the back of a sea turtle. Don't you remember? It was I who gave you a tour of the palace halls and the gardens. It was I who taught you to sing and play piano. It was I who used to play with you every day; all sorts of games. Your favorite has always been hide-and-seek," Eli chuckled and smiled.

Melody stood still, looking down at Eli's tunic to avoid his overwhelming gaze. His words quelled her rebellious spirit like a lullaby quiets an anxious child. In her heart, she knew everything he said was true. She didn't resist as Eli placed a hand under her chin and lifted her face. She was surprised to see tears in his eyes.

"You've been hiding for a very long time, Mel. Won't you come out?"

At his words, Melody was flooded with flashbacks. She saw herself in the palace of Marindel, saying, "How about you count to a thousand while I hide, and then you have to come find me. Sound like fun?"

Eli replied, "Great idea, Mel! I'll go to that corner and get started. One, two, three…" his voice became distant, and she heard him calling, "Melody! Melody, where are you?"

The Serpent said, *You haven't much time. Use your magic to unlock the door. Then come inside, and I will give you power.*

All right. Here I come.

"Melody? Melody!?" Eli's voice called.

Hurry, inside! the Serpent said.

The massive doors slammed shut, silencing Eli's call. The flashback faded with the Serpent's echoing laugh.

Just when she thought it was over, she heard her own voice squeak in the dark, "What in the realm of Tyrizah am I doing?"

"What in the realm of Tyrizah am I doing?" Melody whispered.

And then she broke.

Melody threw her arms around Eli and began to sob.

Eli returned the embrace and rested his face against hers. "It's all right. I'm here. I've found you."

Melody cried into his shoulder until she found the breath and courage to look at him again. She asked in a choked voice, "Why did you come for me?"

Eli took her by the shoulders and said. "Because I love you, Melody. And the Great King loves you, too."

Melody suppressed a sob. "That's impossible. He hates me. I'm a horrible daughter."

"I love you, Melody," he repeated, eyes glimmering. "And the Great King loves you, too."

"But..." Melody's lip quivered.

"Hey!" The big-nosed official yelled. "Get away from her!"

His shout alerted the other officials, who then saw Melody teary-eyed in the arms of Eli. They all shuffled toward her, shouting and waving their arms.

Eli whispered in Melody's ear, "Come find me in the apple orchard tomorrow at sunrise."

Two officials grabbed Eli and tore him away from Melody. They shouted, "What do you think you're doing!? You've offended the queen! Filthy peasant, how dare you!? Where are Tethysian soldiers when we need them? Quick, find the nearest guards! This is grounds for arrest!"

Eli slipped out of their grasp and disappeared into the market-place.

"After him! Don't let him get away!" Several officials ran in pursuit.

Those who stayed behind swarmed around Melody. They wiped her tears, fixed her hair, asked if Eli had done anything malicious, and vowed to ensure he was properly disposed of. She ignored them, watching Eli until he disappeared from sight.

Comprehension

1) Describe Melody's first encounter with Eli. How does she react? How does he respond?

2) When the Serpent attempts to discourage Eli, what does Eli say he has come to do?

3)Why is Eli's mention of hide-and-seek significant?

Reflection

1)Read Luke 15:4-10. Have you ever lost and found something precious to you? How did you feel when you finally found it?

The Prince of Mystery
Summer, 104 IE

Early the next morning, Melody awoke with a start. She remembered the events of the previous day, and a tingling apprehension laced her thoughts. Had Eli really come to find her? Could it even be possible?

There was only one way to find out.

She put on a simple blue tunic and a translucent shawl to cover her head, and she departed quietly. Exiting Diamond City through the eastern gate, she skirted the city wall until she came upon the apple orchard, which sprawled over the nearby hills.

As Melody wandered through the orchard, anxiety welled up in her heart. *What am I doing? This man knows much about Eli and about me, but what if he's a fraud? My officials don't trust him, so maybe I shouldn't either.*

Just then, she realized she was alone.

For the first time in many years, Melody had ventured outside of the palace without anyone to escort her. She began to feel very small and lonely. *What if something bad happens? Something bad* always *hap-*

pens when I'm alone!

Melody peered around as she went. A myriad of birdsongs filled the air, and the dew on the grass reflected the dawning sky. The air was cold and crisp, with a breeze so gentle it was hardly noticeable. The branches stretching overhead were laden with green leaves and ripe pink apples.

Melody took a deep, calming breath as she took in her surroundings. She never realized mornings could be so beautiful. In fact, she tended to sleep in on a regular basis. The anxiety she felt a moment before, dwindled away as she discovered the charm of the early morning.

She quickened her stride as she ascended a hill.

She could tell from the light touching the treetops that the sun was just beginning to rise, and she wanted to get a perfect view.

Once at the summit, Melody was astounded. She had a clear view, not only of the sunrise, but of the entire countryside's rolling green hills speckled with trees and patches of wildflowers. As the sun cleared the horizon, it cast golden rays of light on everything in sight. The drops of dew on the grass twinkled like stars as they reflected the rising sun.

It was the most beautiful thing Melody had seen in a very long time.

"Wonderful, isn't it?" Eli's voice came from somewhere nearby.

Melody gasped and whirled around. There he was, leaning against a tree and looking out at the countryside. The light glistened in his eyes.

"Yes, it's lovely," Melody replied. She fixed her eyes on the landscape, still finding it uncomfortable to look at him.

They watched the sunrise for a moment before Eli asked, "Melody, what do you love about the sun?"

"I, uh…" Melody looked at the ground. Truthfully, she didn't like the sun at all. She never liked being hot, and she hated sweating and getting sunburns. She spoke her mind, "I don't really love anything about it."

"Really?" Eli asked. Melody expected him to mock or judge her in some way, but he didn't. Instead, he asked with genuine interest, "How can you behold a sight as beautiful as this, and not have a single thing come to mind that's lovely about the sun? You did say yourself; it was lovely."

Melody looked again at the countryside. The sun hovered above the horizon, bathing the landscape in golden light. She said, "Well, I do like the way it makes other things look more beautiful."

"Yes, that is a grand quality of the sun, isn't it? More than just aesthetics, the sun gives life to all living things. The plants grow and the flowers bloom because the sun shines on them. It gives warmth and comfort, light and life. It sends water to the sky to become clouds, and when the clouds become dense, the water returns as rain to quench the thirst of the land. Everything we do in this realm is dependent on the sun. We owe it our very lives."

"You sound like a philosopher," Melody said. She realized her tone might have been offensive, so she added, "I mean, not in a bad way. You just know things about the realm, and you talk about them in a way that makes others want to listen."

Eli picked an apple from a branch above him and tossed it to Melody. "Let's sit down for a bit."

She furrowed her brow. "In the wet grass?"

Eli picked an apple for himself and said, "Of course not. Come, this way." He walked a short distance down the hillside to a pile of smooth boulders in the shade of a larger tree. He gestured toward one of the smoothest rocks for Melody to sit on, and he sat cross-legged on one across from her. Once they were both settled, he asked, "Have you ever tried one of these apples before?"

Melody shook her head.

Eli smiled. "Oh, you must! They're the best in the land!"

Melody inspected the large pink apple. It *looked* good, but she was bothered by thoughts of how dirty it must be, and the possibility of worms or parasites inside.

"There's nothing wrong with it," Eli said. "Go on, try it."

She took a bite, and her eyes widened as the flavor exploded in her mouth. Its juicy crunchiness surpassed that of any fruit she could remember!

"Mmmm!" Melody took another bite and chewed voraciously.

Eli chuckled. "Good, huh?"

"Mhmm," Melody replied, taking a third bite.

They enjoyed their apples together in silence for a few moments.

"Ahh," Melody breathed as she threw the core into the grass and leaned back against a neighboring boulder. "That was amazing. I've never had an apple like *that* before."

"Really? Never in your life?"

"Nope. To be honest, I hated apples before you gave me this one."

"How come?"

"I don't know, I just did," Melody shrugged.

"So, you hated apples, and now you don't. And you hated the sun, and now you don't. Is there anything else I can help you un-hate?"

Melody chuckled. "Oh, I don't know. I hate many things. Almost everything. When you've been through as many hard times as I have, it's hard to find a reason to love anything. Much less any*one*."

"Is that a challenge?" Eli asked with a smirk.

"Why do you care?" Melody tried to come off as indifferent, but she couldn't tame the small bit of her heart that rejoiced in how much this man took interest in her.

"I care about everything, and everyone," Eli said, looking out at the countryside. "I care because the Great King cares."

Melody rolled her eyes. "Runs in the family?"

"Not necessarily. To care—that is, to love—is a choice we all have. It's a decision in the face of circumstance. It doesn't matter who you are or what you've been through. Every sentient creature has a choice to love or to hate, to care or to ignore. Ultimately, the state of the realm we live in depends on that choice."

"Given the state of the realm right now, you might be the only person alive who cares."

Eli looked at Melody and said, "You may be right. But that's why I'm here."

"Hm," Melody looked thoughtfully at the ground. Then she stood up and said, "I'm going to get another apple."

Eli shot to his feet and took her hand. "No, no, allow me."

"Hey!" Melody pulled her hand away from his. Then she composed herself and said, "Okay, fine. Just don't touch me."

Eli didn't take offense. He jumped up on a few boulders to reach a branch, picked an apple, and came back to hand it to her. "For you, Milady."

"Don't call me that!" Melody snapped, taking the apple and sitting again. "Everyone and their mother calls me that."

Eli sat as well. "All right. What should I call you, then?"

"Melody's fine." She took a bite of the apple. "Mmmm. Oh, so good! Mmm…"

Eli watched with delight as Melody enjoyed the apple. When she was almost finished, he said, "Melody's a good name."

She acknowledged his reply with a hum as she took one last bite of the apple. Then she said, "You can call me Mel, too, I guess."

Eli smiled and nodded. Then he stood up and said, "Care to take a walk?"

"Maybe. Where to?"

"Jasper Village is just down the hill. I was there a few days ago, and I'd love to show you around."

"*You're* going to show *me* around my own kingdom?"

"Yep. You can't deny you don't get out much, and when you do, how much do you *really* see?"

Melody was offended, so she fumbled for a reason to back out of it. "I don't think I can. My officials are probably wondering where I am, and they'll stress themselves out searching the whole city until they find me."

"Why do they worry so much about you?"

"Because I'm the queen, of course. They keep me safe, they help me make wise decisions, and they help enforce the rules around here."

"Do they care about you?"

"Of *course* they do! Why wouldn't they?"

"Be mindful when you're with them," Eli said. "They're more influential than you think. Though they may seem concerned for your welfare, they're far more concerned with their own prestige."

No, they're not, Melody wanted to say, but something within her kept the words from coming out.

"Come with me," Eli urged, reaching his hand out for Melody to take.

Melody looked from Eli's hand to his beaming face and back again. As much as she didn't want to, the small, untamed part of her heart longed to take his hand and go wherever he took her. It wasn't even so much about the village; she just wanted to be with him.

What? Am I falling in love with him? Melody blushed, struggling to hide her conflicting thoughts and emotions. She had *never* fallen in love before. She hated people far too much for that nonsense. Besides, even if this man standing before her *was* Prince Eli from the Kingdom of Marindel, she'd never been attracted to him in that way. Eli was just a friend and a brother back then.

Of course, he's much older now…and more handsome…

Melody scolded her own heart. *For goodness' sake, control yourself! It's just a casual morning walk. You can do that, can't you?*

She took his hand.

Eli helped her up and said, "All right! Let's go!"

The two of them walked down the hill and skirted the edge of the orchard until they came across a road, and they began traveling north.

Along the way, Melody remained thoughtful. She couldn't decide if she believed this man was Prince Eli. And if he was, what was he doing talking to her? Wouldn't the real Eli be disappointed in her? There's no disputing the fact that she caused the permanent ruin of both Marindel and the realm of Tyrizah by her one mistake. The real Eli would have plenty of reason to hate her.

But still.

This man knew things about her not even Seers had been able to discern. It was like he was there in the beginning, during the Era of Peace, while she grew up in the courts of Marindel. Such knowledge of her past was impossible for anyone except the real Eli.

After all, before this man, only Eli had ever called her Mel.

Melody shook those thoughts out of her head and belittled herself. *What are you thinking, you idiot? There's no way this could be Eli. He's a man, for crying out loud! Eli is supposed to be an elf. How could you even let the possibility cross your mind? He's nothing more than a Seer. A good one, I'll give him that, but a Seer, nonetheless. I know what I'll do: I'll play along with his little ruse and keep him entertained, but I'll be watching and waiting for him to make a mistake. When he does, I'll exploit it to uncover his fraudulent act and have him arrested and killed like every Seer before him. Yes, that's what I'll do.*

"What's on your mind, Mel?" Eli asked.

"Oh, nothing."

Eli stayed silent. When the tension became uncomfortable, Melody sighed and said, "Okay, I'm a bit nervous. Nothing major. It just comes with walking alone with a stranger to a random village when you're the queen and many people don't like you."

"You're afraid to trust me," Eli said.

Melody tensed. In five words, Eli effectively summarized her entire dilemma. *He's one hell of a good Seer,* she thought.

Eli said, "I understand what troubles you, and that's why I'm taking you to Jasper Village. If you're willing, come and see for yourself that I am who I say I am, and more importantly, believe what I've come to tell you."

"What if I'm not willing?" Melody challenged.

"I won't force you to come. You can go back to the palace whenever you'd like."

Melody was surprised Eli didn't sound angry. She was used to others reacting in fear or anger when she tried to be difficult, but thus far, Eli had only treated her graciously. As she thought about it, the part of her heart that was fascinated with him grew a teeny bit larger.

No! Melody rebuked herself and repressed her emotions. *Perhaps I should turn back now, lest I be seduced by him and betrayed in the end! That's what men do, after all!* But even as she considered it, she realized how ridiculous her thoughts were in light of what she knew about Eli's—or whoever he was's—character.

Finally, she made her decision. "I'll come with you for now, but at noon I'm going back to Diamond City."

"Very well," Eli said, smiling. "I'll enjoy your company for as long as you choose to stay."

The two of them reached Jasper Village soon after their discussion. In total, they had only been walking for half an hour.

The road ran through the center of the village, and most of the buildings were aligned on either side. There were many people bustling about, and Melody groaned at the thought of being surrounded by commoners. On the far side of the village was an imposing stone tower, adorned with black banners featuring the insignia of the Empire: a silver dragon with a gold spear.

"What's so special about this village?" Melody asked.

"You'll see."

"I don't see anything," Melody said under her breath.

A few seconds later, an excited little boy scampered toward them. "Mister Eli! You're back!"

"Hey there, buddy!" Eli said, stooping down to meet his flying hug head-on. He stood and lifted the boy into the air, who laughed with glee.

Melody stood by with a stupefied look on her face.

Eli put the child down, who turned and ran toward a pregnant woman who was approaching them. "Mommy! Eli's back!"

"I see that, dear!" the mother replied. Then, smiling at Eli, she said, "It's so good to see you again!"

"And you as well, Trisha," Eli replied.

A man followed Trisha, holding a little girl who looked a couple years older than the boy. He said, "Welcome back, Eli! Are you hungry? We're just cooking breakfast, and we'd love to have you."

"Auben, that's very kind of you!" Eli looked at Melody and asked, "Are you hungry, Mel? What do you think?"

Melody couldn't speak. Who were these people? How did they know each other? And why were they offering to feed Eli?

Just then, the little boy approached her and looked up with a blank expression. "Who are you?"

"Who am *I*?" Melody asked, taken aback. She looked up at the boy's parents and sister, who also stared blankly at her. She looked down at the boy, then at Eli, then back at the parents. Exasperated, she said, "Don't tell me none of you know who I am!"

"We've never met, have we?" Trisha asked. "Are you a friend of Eli's?"

"Of course we haven't met, but how could you not know who I am? I'm Melody, the Queen of Rhema!"

The parents' eyes widened.

Auben fumbled for words, "Well, um, greetings, Your Majesty. Please forgive our ignorance."

"I didn't know we had a queen," the boy said. "I thought we had an emperor. Are you the emperor's wife?"

"Trevor, come here," Trisha beckoned. To Melody, she said, "I'm sorry we didn't recognize you, miss. We've never seen you before, that's all."

Melody's pride was wounded. She couldn't believe these commoners had no idea who she was. She was also indignant that their son believed the Tethysian emperor was the sole ruler of Rhema.

Eli broke the silence by properly introducing her. "My friends, this is Melody, the Queen of Rhema. I've brought her here to meet you and to show her around the village."

"Oh, that's wonderful," Trisha replied, forcing a smile. "Will both of you join us for breakfast? We'd be honored."

"No, thank you," Melody said. "I'm not hungry. Besides, I have to get going at noon. Eli, we'd better keep moving if you want to show me around the village."

Eli looked at Melody with a glimmer of sadness, but he nodded and said, "All right. Thank you, Trisha. Another time."

"Aw!" Trevor shouted. "Mister Eli, don't let her ruin your fun!"

"Hey!" Melody snapped.

Eli put a hand on Melody's shoulder and said to Trevor, "It's all right, bud, I'll be back soon. I promise we'll spend a whole afternoon playing together. How's that?"

"Okay!" Trevor ran and hugged his father's leg.

"Eli, before you go," Auben said, "I want to thank you again for saving our daughter's life. If it weren't for you, Lia wouldn't be alive today." He looked endearingly at the girl he held in his arms.

Eli smiled and nodded. "She's very precious, and the Great King loves her very much."

"Please come back soon!" Trisha said. "We would love to hear more about you and the Great King. Our home is always open to you!"

"Of course, I look forward to it! Good day, all of you!"

The family waved goodbye as Eli and Melody continued further into the village.

Once the family was out of earshot, Melody took Eli's arm to stop him from walking. She spoke sternly, "What in the kingdom of Rhema was that all about!?"

"They're good friends of mine, that's all. They saw me and came to say hello."

"How do you know them? You're an outsider! You came here from…somewhere, be it Marindel or another place. Yet somehow, they had no idea who I was! That is unacceptable! Embarrassing! Humiliating!"

"Melody." The authority in Eli's voice quieted her. "I stayed a couple days in Jasper Village before I arrived in Diamond City to find you. That family invited me into their home, and I stayed the night. We got to know each other very well. Melody, when was the last time you went to a village to spend time with the people there? To get to know them and understand their way of life?"

Melody was too stubborn to answer. She would never lower herself to the level of a commoner. It was unthinkable.

"What I want you to see," Eli said, putting his hands on her shoulders and looking into her eyes, "is that these people are loved and valued by the Great King. They are worthy of being loved and valued by you, by me, and by everyone. You must not think yourself higher simply because you're a queen. Even the Great King, the greatest ruler of all, spent time with the common people. The Serpent has brought much hatred into this realm, but I have come to set an example for you and for others who will believe in me."

Melody avoided eye contact with Eli. She squirmed out of his grasp and pouted.

"Mel, I'm not disappointed in you. I know how hard it is for you to understand these things. All you need is a bit of time, and there's nothing wrong with that. Besides, I'm not finished showing you around yet."

Melody remained silent.

"Come on, cheer up," Eli said, gently brushing her cheek.

She finally made eye contact with him. The intensity of his gaze made her heart skip a beat.

"There's more to see," Eli said with an adventurous glimmer in his eye. "Let's go!"

She nodded. Most of the stubbornness in her heart melted away, and she felt peace. Deep down, she greatly appreciated Eli's patience and tact. No one had ever shown her this much kindness before.

As they continued to walk, Eli reached out and took her hand.

This time, Melody didn't refuse him.

As they went along the main village road, people greeted Eli from left and right. Melody was surprised he was so well-known for only having stayed in the village for two days. He must have said or done something extraordinary to get the whole village's attention. As she thought more about it, a possibility came to mind that piqued her interest. Remembering the transformation of the pineapples Eli caused in Diamond City, she asked, "Eli, what did you do to save that family's daughter?"

"Ah," Eli smiled as he recalled the memory. "On the day I arrived, Lia had been sick for a week with a high fever, vomiting, and tremors. She wasn't responding to treatment, and the medic said she would die very soon. When I heard about it, I went to see her for myself, and my heart was broken. I knew Lia was a victim of the Serpent's cruelty, so I placed my hand on her forehead and sang of my father's love for her and his desire that she be healed. When I finished, she was well."

"That's incredible," Melody replied. "So, you *do* have some sort of powers after all!"

Eli shook his head. "I have no power of my own. I knew my father the King wanted to heal Lia, so I responded in obedience to his will. His power healed her, not mine."

Melody scoffed, "Would you say his power healed the pineapples, too?"

"Yes," Eli agreed. "Whether it involves pineapples or people, the Great King lets those who love and obey him tap into his power to create opportunities for others to get to know him."

Melody was puzzled. "What do you mean?"

"For example, when Lia was healed, quite naturally, everyone was shocked. Just like you assumed, they thought I had magical powers. I took the opportunity to tell them about the Great King and his love for them. Most were touched by what I had to say. Some weren't; they thought I was a lunatic. Regardless, everyone can now call to mind the time when a little girl, destined to die, was healed by a humble nobody who came along at the right time and sent the sickness fleeing in the name of the Great King."

Just as Eli finished speaking, someone up ahead shouted, "Well, well, if it isn't the sorcerer of Marindel!"

Melody looked and saw five Tethysian soldiers coming down the opposite side of the road. She tensed at the sight of them.

"Captain Matthias," Eli greeted the leading officer.

"Hmph," Matthias flicked his chin as he came closer. "You've got some nerve, coming back here after what you did."

"Leave him alone," Melody said, standing between Eli and the incoming soldiers.

"Shut up, Princess," Matthias said as he barged past her. The other soldiers surrounded Eli, their expressions proud and scoffing. The captain asked Eli, "What did we tell you about showing your face around here again?"

"I answer only to my father, the Great King."

"Don't give us that phony gimmick again! You're no prince, you don't come from no King, and you don't belong here in Rhema. This is your last chance, so listen up. Take your magic tricks out of here pronto, or you'll face the tooth and claw of the Tethysian Law."

The other soldiers chuckled.

"I love that rhyme," one of them said.

Matthias elbowed that soldier.

Eli stood confidently and said, "You so-called protectors of the land are selfish and proud. You have no regard for the plight of the people of Rhema, and when someone comes to meet their needs, you chase them out. Is there *any* bit of kindness in you?"

"See here, you ignorant little—" Matthias was cut off as Eli spoke over him, "The Serpent will treat you just as you treat those under you unless you turn to the Great King, follow his ways, and trust in him."

"I've killed serpents uglier than you with this very sword, so mind your words!" Matthias placed a hand on the hilt of his weapon. "In the name of Emperor Flavian the Bright, ruler of the Tethysian Empire, you are under arrest!"

Before Matthias finished speaking, Eli slipped between the soldiers and ran. "Come on, Mel!"

Melody had been standing off to the side, unsure of what to do. When Eli called, she ran after him.

"Get him!" Matthias yelled. He and his soldiers gave chase.

Eli slowed enough for Melody to catch up, and he took her hand

and led the way through the busy village streets.

"Why are you provoking Tethysian soldiers!?" Melody asked, panting for breath as she kept Eli's pace.

"Sometimes standing up for what's right will provoke those who seek to exploit others for their own gain," Eli replied.

"But they're *Tethysian soldiers*! You know they can kill you, right!?"

"They can kill me, but they can't challenge truth and expect to win!"

"You're crazy!"

"Maybe just a little!"

Eli turned and took Melody through a small alley between two buildings, scattering a flock of chickens as they passed. Emerging from the other side in a flurry of feathers, Eli ran toward the Tethysian fortress on the far side of the village.

Melody dug her heels into the ground. "We can't go that way! That's their fortress!"

Eli stopped and looked at her. "Do you trust me, Mel?"

"Not really!"

"There he is!" Matthias' voice called from the mouth of the alley they just passed through.

Melody panicked and yelled, "Okay, yes! Yes, I trust you!" "All right, let's go!" Eli ran toward the fortress with a panting Melody in tow.

The soldiers emerged from the alley single-file and chased after them. There were fewer people walking about the closer they came to the fortress, so it became harder for Eli and Melody to stay hidden.

When they were around fifty feet away from the entrance, Eli turned left and went down another alley. This one was much longer and led to a smaller street, from which many more alleys branched off. Eli led Melody through the maze, zigzagging this way and that.

"Where'd he go?" a soldier shouted.

"Let's split up!"

"Flush him out!"

The soldiers went down separate alleys with the hope of trapping Eli, but to no avail.

Eli and Melody soon emerged from the alleys and found themselves running through a field of tall grass at the edge of the village. The Tethysian fortress was to their right. In front of them were only a few buildings and fences separating them from the sprawling Rhema countryside.

"Where do we go now?" Melody asked.

"We'll lose them in the group of mansions ahead," Eli replied.

Melody wasn't sure what Eli was getting at, but she didn't see the point in arguing.

They passed between the first two buildings, and Eli immediately turned right. They headed toward a manor, and Melody looked up to see a Tethysian banner hanging above the door.

"We're not going in there, are we?" Melody asked.

"Yes, we are!"

"You're crazy! That's a *Tethysian* manor!" Melody pulled her hand out of Eli's grasp. "Let's go around it! We can hide in the tall grass just beyond." Without waiting for his response, she changed course and began circumventing the building.

"Melody! Wait!" Eli called, running after her.

"I know what I'm doing! Just follow me!"

She approached a wooden fence attached to the back corner of the building. With some effort, she jumped and hauled herself over it.

"Wait! Melody, stop!"

When Melody landed on the other side of the fence, she broke into a sprint. There was only a short stretch of grass in front of her, then one more fence, and then freedom.

I'm gonna make it! We're gonna make it! This is exhilarating! Melody grinned. She'd never had this much fun running from trouble before.

An angry growl banished her cavalier thoughts.

No! Not a guard dog! Melody looked aside, expecting to see a dog running after her. But what she saw instead caused her heart to skip a beat.

A vibrant orange dragon crouched thirty feet away, looking straight at her. It was snarling and pawing the ground, ready to pounce.

Comprehension

1) How do you think Eli uses the sun and the apples to show Melody aspects of his own character?

2) What plan does Melody come up with to justify her walk with Eli?

3) Why is Melody frustrated with Eli's friends in Jasper Village?

4) While being chased by soldiers, what happens to Melody when she goes her own way instead of following Eli?

Reflection

1) Read Psalm 139:1-16. Have you ever been surprised by how perfectly God knows you? Maybe it came in the form of something you saw or read at the right time, or someone who encouraged you with exactly the right words. How did it make you feel?

6

The Prince of Wonder
Summer, 104 IE

When she saw the dragon, Melody screamed and ran away from it. The dragon yowled and bounded after her faster than any guard dog could ever hope to run.

There was no way she'd escape in time.

When the dragon was a second away from snatching Melody, Eli tackled her to the ground. The dragon soared overhead, buffeting the two of them with its wings and sending them tumbling together through the grass. Even after they stopped moving, Melody clung to Eli with her eyes squeezed shut.

"Mel, are you all right?" Eli whispered.

"No!" Melody trembled. "Eli, there's a dragon! A *dragon!*"

"I know. Hang on, watch this." Eli stood to his feet.

The dragon had turned and was facing them again, its head low and wings spread wide, tail lashing like a cat's. It was small for a dragon, but still twice the size of a horse; limber and muscular. It was orange, as

Melody observed earlier, with a golden underside and maroon tiger-like stripes across the length of its body and wings. Its tail had fan-like appendages for enhanced flight. Its face was smooth and aerodynamic.

Eli wasn't the least bit intimidated by the dragon. He walked toward it and began to sing.

Melody stayed low, afraid to do anything but watch.

The dragon hissed at Eli, arching its back and pawing the ground.

Eli sang louder.

His voice tugged at Melody's heart. Eli was singing in Elvish, a language she had long since forgotten, but the sound of it filled her heart with peace.

The dragon inched closer to Eli, still growling and poised to attack.

Eli was undeterred. He sang beautifully, looked the dragon in the eyes, and extended his hand toward it.

As the gap between them closed, the dragon's eyes softened, and its wings folded.

No way, Melody thought as she looked on.

The dragon's head swayed back and forth to the lilt of Eli's song. The closer he got, the more relaxed the dragon became. When Eli reached the dragon with his hand stretched out, it chirped and pushed its muzzle against his palm.

Eli smiled. "There you go, boy." Then he called over his shoulder, "Come here, Mel, it's all right!"

Melody stood and approached them. "Are you sure?"

When the dragon noticed her, it hissed.

"Ah!" Melody flinched. "Eli, it still hates me!"

"Whoa, hey," Eli said, rubbing the dragon's neck. "You'll have to sing for it. Remember how I taught you?"

"No," Melody retorted. "I don't sing, and you never taught me to sing."

"Yes, I did. You don't remember?"

"No."

"I *know* you can do it. You have the most beautiful voice!"

"Oh, you're talking about teaching me to sing in Marindel, aren't you?" Melody scoffed. "Well, of course, I don't remember now. It was *so* long ago!"

"I know you can." Eli removed his hands from the dragon and backed away.

The dragon faced Melody and crouched low with a growl.

"Eli, what are you doing!?"

"Come on, I won't let it attack you. Trust me."

Melody gulped. She murmured in a sing-songy voice, "I'm looking at a dragon, a really scary dragon, that wants to bite my face off—"

The dragon yowled and pawed the ground, flaring its wings out.

"Different song, Mel!" Eli called. "Remember how I taught you!"

"I don't remember, okay!?"

"Yes, you do! I believe in you!"

The dragon yowled again, preparing to pounce.

Remember, remember, remember! Melody didn't know how to remember something like that, but she had to!

She thought about how Eli sang. It had a quality unlike any song she had ever heard. She closed her eyes and imagined she could hear it. She focused on an image of Eli singing in a garden with fountains, looking at her with a sweet and tender gaze. This was the son of the Great King. Her brother. Her best friend.

"Let it flow," Eli had said. "Don't think about the words. Just focus on the Great King. Think about how much he loves you. Let your heart rejoice in the freedom of knowing who you are and whose you are."

She remembered.

With hardly another thought, she opened her mouth and began to sing. She could hardly believe what was coming out of her mouth! Elvish words she didn't know she remembered, knitted together in the most wonderful tune! Remembering what Eli did before, she walked toward the dragon with her hand outstretched.

The dragon calmed down quickly. Before Melody could even place her hand on its head, it rolled over and exposed its belly for her to pet.

Eli chuckled. "I think it likes you more than me!"

"What's going on out here?" a voice called. It belonged to a middle-aged Tethysian man who stood bewildered at the back doorway of the manor. "What did you folks just do to my dragon? And, my lawn…!"

"The lawn?" Melody looked at the grass around her and saw it was speckled with purple flowers. "Whoa, did I do that?"

"You sure did," Eli said, walking over to stand beside her. He looked at the Tethysian man and said, "Good to see you again, Caruso."

"And you as well, Eli," Caruso said with a nod. "Though, I'm perplexed as to why you've intruded upon my dragon keep. If you wanted to say hello to Hunter, all you had to do was knock and ask."

"It's my fault," Melody said. "We were running from soldiers who wanted to arrest Eli. Friends of yours, maybe. I thought this would be the fastest way to the tall grass on the other side, but I didn't know there was a dragon here. I'm sorry."

Eli looked proudly at Melody and put his arm around her.

"No friend of mine wants to arrest Eli, I'll say that," Caruso replied. "This man helped me a great deal a few days ago. I would never accuse him of any treachery."

"Even though he healed a girl?" Melody tested. "Even though he says he's a Prince from Marindel? And his father is the Great King?"

"Noted, and irrelevant. Now, can you please explain what you did to Hunter? He's acting like a kitten!"

Melody looked at Eli. "What happened to the dragon, Eli?"

"We tamed him with the Music of Marindel. A song of wonder and reverence unto the Great King."

Caruso blinked. "I have no idea what that means, but it seems effective. No Tethysian has ever tamed a dragon like that, especially not a dracoviper. They're very loyal and territorial."

Eli nodded. "Dracovipers are also perceptive. They realize quickly whether a person is a friend or foe. Anyone with an honest heart can tame a dracoviper with ease. I can tell he respects you."

"Hm," Caruso smiled at the compliment. "Hunter here could fly away at any time and never come back, but he knows his place is here with me. I never have to worry about leashing or caging him." He paused for a moment, stroking his stubbly chin. "Can you teach me? The music, I mean?"

"The Music of Marindel is not yet for the creatures of the surface to know. However, a time is soon coming when it will be available to every one of the Great King's followers."

"Hmm…" Caruso was completely clueless. He shrugged and said, "Well, since you two are here, you can give me a hand. I have a talongrunt dragon on the other side of the fence there, and she's got a nasty temper. Could you tame her, too? I'd appreciate it."

"I think we've seen enough dragons for one day," Melody said, turning to walk away.

Eli held her close and said, "No, let's have a look."

Caruso led Eli and Melody to the other side of the yard, where there was a gate in the fence. He pulled out a key to open the lock and then opened the door to peek inside. He said, "She's leashed up, but that won't stop her from breathing fire. Don't aggravate her."

Eli looked at Melody and asked, "Do you think you can handle her?"

Melody quickly shook her head.

"Come on, Mel, I know you can!"

Melody threw her hands up. "Why do we have to do this, anyway? What's the point?"

"You'll see. Trust me."

Melody looked desperately at Eli. "You're making it very difficult for me to trust you."

Eli smiled in return. "I *know* you can do it. Don't be afraid, I'll be right here."

Melody steadied her beating heart with a deep breath. *Fine. If he wants to see me tame a dragon, then I'm gonna tame a dragon. I'll show him.* Then she said, "Okay, I'm going. But be ready to save me if something happens."

"Of course," Eli nodded.

"All right. Here I go," Melody stepped through the door and into the talongrunt's pen.

It didn't take long to locate the dragon, which was leashed with a chain to a thick post in the back corner of the pen. A bit larger than Hunter, she was bird-like in appearance, with two sturdy hind legs, wings instead of forearms, a whip-like tail, and a swan-like neck with a small head. She was green and scaly, rougher-looking than the dracoviper. And as the dragon's name insinuated, she had fearsome black talons.

"Her name is Kaya," Caruso said.

"Kaya. Suits her well," Melody muttered as she beheld the dragon.

When Kaya saw Melody, she straightened her posture and flared her wings out, squawking a warning.

All right. Time to sing. Melody closed her eyes and tried to focus on her memory of Eli from earlier. A second later, she heard Eli yell, "Look out!"

Melody opened her eyes in time to see Kaya spit a ball of flame in her direction.

"Ah!" Melody jumped back, narrowly escaping the fire, and stumbled backward onto the ground.

"Stay alert!" Caruso called. "I wasn't kidding about her temper!"

"Thanks for the warning," Melody grumbled, standing up. She looked at the black scar on the ground where the fire had burned the grass, and then she looked at the wooden fence and the wooden manor. "Caruso, why do you keep an angry, fire-breathing dragon in a pen made of wood?"

"It's Tamaha wood. Fireproof."

"Oh, you've thought of everything, haven't you?"

"Come on, Mel, give it another try!" Eli said.

"All right, all right," Melody looked again at Kaya. When the two made eye contact, Kaya squawked and bared her needle-like teeth.

"Stop it, Kaya!" Melody shouted. "Bad girl!"

Kaya shot another fireball at Melody, who was better prepared for it this time and ran out of the way. She went closer and said, "Kaya, stop!"

Kaya tried to charge Melody, but the chain leash held her back. Her claws scored deep gouges in the dirt as she pulled on the chain.

"Isn't she supposed to sing?" Caruso asked Eli.

He didn't answer. He was intently watching Melody.

"Kaya, calm down," Melody said.

Kaya shot another fireball, and Melody dodged it just in time. She wasn't fazed by the danger anymore; she boldly approached the dragon. "Kaya, calm down!"

Kaya took a step back with an angry squawk.

Melody stopped a dozen feet away and said, "I'm not afraid of you."

The dragon growled in defiance, tugging to escape from the chain.

Melody took a deep breath and began to sing, just like she did earlier.

She didn't appear responsive to the song.

Melody stopped and said, "Eli, it's not working!"

"Keep going! You can do it!"

Melody continued. While she did so, the burnt scars on the grass began to heal.

Kaya's behavior changed slowly. She stopped tugging at the chain. She threatened to shoot fire, with smoke steaming from her nostrils, but the song's calming magic quenched her aggression. She squawked and stomped with frustration.

"Just a little more," Eli said.

Caruso was watching with eyes wide.

As Melody continued singing, she walked closer.

Kaya folded her wings and lowered her head. Her expression was still hostile, but the battle in her mind was evident. Soon the dragon crouched, wrapped her tail around herself, and looked down at the ground.

Melody moved to place her hand on Kaya's snout, but she recoiled with a stubborn grunt. Melody said, "It's all right, you can trust me. I'm not going to hurt you."

Kaya looked at Melody from the corner of her eyes.

"You're so silly, you know that?" Melody cracked a grin. "Come on, let me pet you."

Kaya groaned and lowered her head but still kept it just out of Melody's reach.

Meanwhile, Eli had walked over and stood behind her. He said, "Tell Kaya you love her."

Melody glanced at Eli, and after a pause, she said to the dragon,

"Kaya, I love you."

Though Melody's demeanor was nowhere near as gentle and kind as Eli's, Kaya was perceptive enough to realize Melody's words were truthful. With a hesitant warble, she craned her neck forward and touched her snout to Melody's hand.

Melody smiled and giggled, reaching up to stroke Kaya's jawline. "See? That wasn't so bad! What took you so long?"

Eli chuckled. "Well done!"

"Thanks!" Melody turned and shoved Eli playfully. "But I still think you're crazy for making me do that."

"Hey," Eli grinned. "I sought only to call out the strong, brave woman I know you are."

"I could've died, you know."

"I knew you wouldn't. I'll never put you through something you can't handle."

Melody failed to restrain a blush.

"You two wanna take them out for a ride?" Caruso asked. "They haven't had a chance to stretch their wings in a few days."

Eli looked up at the sun. "I'm not sure we have the time. It's almost noon, and Melody would like to be in Diamond City by then. We should start heading back."

Melody was overcome with regret at Eli's response. He was right; it was indeed almost noon. She'd wanted to go back to the palace to alleviate any potential concerns of her officials, who didn't know she'd gone out to meet Eli. She was just beginning to enjoy his company, and her appreciation of him was growing by the hour. Plus, she was still very curious to find out if he was right in claiming to be the Eli of Marindel, the Great Prince of the Sea. Part of her still doubted his claims, and she was still paying close attention to his words and actions to find fault in him. But the more she spent time with him, the more she believed.

Surely my officials can't be too worried about me yet, Melody thought. *If Eli really is the Great Prince, they would be amiss to be upset with me for spending time with him. It would be in our best interest for me to continue investigating this matter, so when I return to the palace, I can give them a clear answer about his identity. Who knows? If all of this works out, and I eventually come to…marry him…* She blushed at the thought. *Perhaps we'll become strong enough to resist the Tethysian Empire. We can do away with them forever.*

"What do you think, Mel? Would you like to start heading back?"

Melody smiled and said, "Nah, I don't need to go back yet. Wouldn't you rather show me around the rest of Rhema? What's one village compared to the whole kingdom?"

Eli's eyes glowed with delight. "I would be honored."

"I'll ready the saddles then," Caruso said with a nod. "Would you like anything to drink in the meantime?"

"Water, please," Melody replied.

"Got it," Caruso turned and went back into his manor.

Melody leaned up against Kaya and stroked her head. The talongrunt responded by closing her eyes and purring gently. After a moment Melody asked, "Eli, do you remember when you asked what else you can help me un-hate?"

"Yep. What about it?"

"Well, I think dragons are growing on me. They've attacked me many times before; I've had too many near-death experiences to count. I've considered them monsters, and I think most people in the realm would agree with me." She looked at Eli while stroking Kaya's neck. "But I never knew they could be friendly if you treated them right. They even have personalities, like house pets."

"Like people, even," Eli added.

Caruso returned, bringing two glasses of water. After handing them off, he said, "I'll saddle up Hunter first. I'll be back for Kaya."

Melody took a big sip of water and said, "I think dragons may be easier to tame than people."

"Is that so?"

"Mhmm," Melody nodded. "People don't change. They're mostly horrible, with a tiny speck of goodness here and there. The speck is so small, it doesn't count in the end. People *say* nice things, but they *do* horrible things. It's been that way for as long as I can remember."

"What makes you say that?"

"Well, it's true, isn't it?"

"Perhaps," Eli poked Melody on the forehead. "What do you see in yourself?"

She paused, frowning slightly. "I'm horrible. And don't you dare say I'm not."

"I won't argue with you," Eli said, much to her surprise. He went on without any hint of condescension. "You're prideful and stubborn. You look to serve yourself, with no regard for the needs of others. However, I see your pain and the lies the Serpent has woven into your soul from the very beginning. Remember how you approached Kaya in a way that diffused her temper, so you could make peace with her? She reminds you of yourself, does she not? That's why you share a connection with her."

Melody listened thoughtfully.

"I see the speck of goodness in your heart, Mel. And I believe in its potential to grow and triumph."

Melody sighed. "You are an extremely complicated individual."

"Eli!" Caruso called, holding a saddle and running up to them. "There are soldiers at the door looking for you. Here's Kaya's saddle, and here's the key to unleash her. I'll keep 'em busy, and you two fly out of here as soon as you can. Got it?"

Eli received the items. "Will do. Thank you for all your help."

"I'm only returning the favor," Caruso said with a nod before going back into the manor.

As Melody watched him go, she asked, "How did you help Caruso?"

Eli told the story while saddling Kaya. "When I was in town a couple days ago, he was in the general store looking to buy supplies, and the shop owner and some of the customers were giving him a hard time. One of your officials was there, too, instigating the whole thing. They didn't want to sell anything to him because he's a wealthy, dragon-own-ing Tethysian. I came in as they were arguing, and I diffused the situation. One cannot rightly classify all Tethysians as imperial overlords. Caruso has a good heart, as you've seen, and I helped the people in the shop understand that. The only person who wasn't happy in the end was your official, who left when the shop owner agreed to do business with Caruso."

"It's a good thing you showed up before any Tethysian soldiers did. That would've ended badly."

"Agreed," Eli said, just then releasing Kaya from her leash. "Speaking of soldiers, Kaya's ready to ride. Would you like to take her or Hunter?"

Melody's eye twinkled. "Who's faster?"

"Definitely, Hunter." Eli raised an eyebrow. "Are you *sure* you want to take the faster dragon?"

"Yes!"

Having heard his name, Hunter leapt over the fence and landed proudly in front of Melody.

"Whoa!" Melody jumped in surprise.

Just then, they heard Matthias shout, "I hear someone in the back! Don't tell me no one's here. I *know* there is! You're acting in defiance of the Imperial Law!"

"Hurry," Eli whispered. "We have to move."

"Okay." Melody clambered onto Hunter's back. "Wait, Eli, how do I ride a dragon?"

"It's a bit like riding a horse."

"But there are no reins."

"See the handles in front of the saddle, strapped to his neck? Hold on to those and tilt to turn. He'll take care of the rest."

"All right," Melody grabbed the handles.

"Now tell him to fly," Eli said. "You go ahead."

The sound of a door flinging open preceded a soldier's voice, "The dragon's missing!"

"Ahhh! Fly!" Melody shouted in panic.

Hunter took a short running start and bounded into the sky with a powerful thrust of his wings. Melody screamed, unprepared for how fast Hunter could really fly.

"Come on, Kaya! Let's go!" Eli and Kaya took off after Hunter.

Matthias and his men charged into Kaya's pen seconds later. Matthias stomped his foot. "Damn! They got away!"

Caruso stumbled in after them, feigning surprise as he saw the dragons flying off in the distance. "Oh my, they've taken the dragons. I'm sorry, sir, they must've jumped the fence. You were right all along."

"Of *course* I was right," Matthias grumbled, heading back toward the manor.

"What, might I ask, are you going to do with them when you catch them?"

"We'll make him pay. With his life, if necessary."

"He hasn't done something deserving of death, has he?"

Matthias whirled around and snapped, "Use your brain, you aristocratic twit! He practices sorcery and claims to be some sort of Great Prince! The commoners are fascinated with him, and do you know what that means?"

"I'm sure if you talk with him, you'll see—"

"It means he's up to no good! In the name of Emperor Flavian the Bright, I will see to it that he is silenced before he turns the hearts of this kingdom against the Tethysian Empire."

Caruso remained calm. "All right. What will you do with the queen, then?"

"Hmph. Once her valiant vigilante is out of the way, she will once again be a pawn in the hands of the governor."

Caruso frowned, hardly able to contain his dismay. He cleared his throat and said, "Well then, you'd better get moving if you hope to catch them. Can I get you and your men anything to drink on your way out?"

Comprehension

1) How does Eli tame the dragon?

2) What memory helps Melody reclaim her ability to sing in Elvish? What were Eli's instructions?

3) Why does Melody change her mind about returning to Diamond City at noon?

4) What comparison does Eli draw between Melody and Kaya?

Reflection

1) Are there any hobbies that you've neglected since you've gotten older? Have you rediscovered any of them? If so, describe the experience. If not, ask the Lord if there's anything He would like to re-teach you and write it down.

The Prince of Legend
Summer, 104 IE

Hunter soared into the sky, pumping his wings and relishing every moment of his airborne freedom.

Melody held the handles for dear life, crouched low and cringing with fear. The shawl that had been covering her head now trailed behind like a scarf, and her curly hair was a frazzled mess. "Hunter! Slow down!" She cried.

Hunter grunted in apology and relaxed his energetic pace, leveling out and allowing the wind to carry him forward.

"Much better," Melody said, though she remained tense.

A moment later, Kaya and Eli caught up to them. "I told you he was fast. Did he surprise you?"

"Just a bit," Melody said, sitting up straight to look unafraid. "I've never gone so fast before, that's all."

"It's all right. You've never flown a dragon, and I'd say you're already doing well for your first try."

"Thanks."

Eli took a deep breath and spread his arms wide. "Look at this view! Have you ever seen the kingdom of Rhema from this high up?"

Melody looked down. At first, she felt a nervous cringe in the pit of her stomach, but she quickly realized what Eli was talking about. Rolling green hills stretched below and around them in every direction, dotted with small trees and laced with dirt roads. A few villages were visible from this high up, as well as some distant wooded areas. Diamond City was beneath them as a sprawling stone maze, glistening in the noonday sun. Jasper Village was small in comparison. The sky was dotted with plump, white clouds, which cast moving shadows upon the landscape. Melody held her breath as she beheld her kingdom. "Eli, it's beautiful!"

"You've lived here for hundreds of years and never thought to ride across the kingdom on a dragon?" Eli chuckled. "Well, I'm honored to be your guide for the day. Hang on to those handles and follow me!" With that, Eli urged Kaya to fly higher and faster.

Melody was buffeted by a gust of wind from Kaya's wings as they passed over her. She told Hunter, "Don't let us fall behind!"

Hunter grunted and turned upward, once again pounding the air with his wings.

The two of them flew higher and higher until they were level with the clouds. They flew all around and between them, the dragons' wings gracing the edges and sending spurts of mist into the air. Eli whooped and hollered, directing Kaya to swoop up and down with corkscrews and loops. Melody didn't participate, but she enjoyed watching Eli have so much fun. She even recalled vague memories of Eli performing all sorts of tricks and maneuvers throughout the flooded palace of Marindel.

Eli has always been a thrill-seeker, Melody thought with a smile. *Never timid. Always bold and ready to try something new.*

Hunter looked back at Melody and tilted his head.

"What? ...Oh, no, I'd rather not join in."

"Hey, Mel," Eli said as Kaya pulled up underneath them. He was reclining on her back with his hands behind his head, legs crossed. "You feeling all right? Come on, let's have some fun!"

"I'm fine, thanks," Melody replied.

"Are you sure? You can't keep Hunter forever, you know. This might be our only chance to fly dragons together."

"I, uh..." Melody trailed off. She understood what Eli was saying, and part of her wanted to throw fear into the wind and have fun with him, just like they did when they were kids. But another part of her, a significantly larger part, remembered what happened the last time she played a game with Eli. Melody cringed and shook her head. "I'm sorry, I can't."

"I'll be here with you," Eli said. "You can trust me. I wouldn't ask you to do anything too dangerous."

Melody took more time to think about it.

"It's your choice," Eli said, sitting up and shrugging. "But it won't be as much fun without you."

"Well, I..." Melody looked down at the ground again. They were higher up now than the last time she looked, and she shuddered.

Hunter grumbled impatiently.

"All right, all right. I trust you." Melody looked down at Eli, made eye contact, and said again, "I trust you."

"Very well, then!" Eli grinned, braced himself in the saddle, and patted Kaya on the neck. "All right, girl, let's go!"

Kaya screeched and dove into a downward spiral.

"Hunter," Melody gulped. "Please be careful."

Hunter yowled and plummeted after Kaya. Melody screamed the entire way down.

The two dragons ended their dive with an upward swoop, careening into a large cloud. When they shot out the other side, Eli was whooping joyfully, and Melody's scream had evolved into a nervous laugh.

Kaya did a corkscrew and then plummeted down, folding her wings and legs close to her body to enable the fastest possible descent.

"Oh no," Melody said as she watched Kaya. "Hunter, please, no."

Hunter looked back at Melody with one mischievous eye and then turned in a corkscrew to dive after Kaya.

Once again, Melody screamed.

Hunter, more aerodynamic than Kaya, was able to catch up. As they sped past, Eli said, "Having fun yet!?"

"I'm trying!" Melody shouted mid-scream.

"Stop trying and just enjoy it!"

They were descending fast. A jagged coastline was beneath them, with crashing waves and sharp rocks awaiting their arrival.

Melody yelled, "Hunter, pull up!"

Hunter swooped into level flight just before hitting the ocean. With extreme speed, he turned sideways to avoid a jutting rock spire and then curved in closer to the water flying parallel to a breaching wave. His wing gently graced the inside of it. Seawater sprinkled Melody's face as they went.

"I will not be afraid of this," Melody declared to herself. "If Eli's not afraid, there's no reason I should be!"

Hunter cleared the wave and flew up over a cliff topped with thick woodland. He skimmed above the canopy, only several feet above the tallest trees, and looked back at Melody.

"What? Are you wondering if I'm having fun, too?"

Hunter shook his neck, wiggling the handles of the saddle. Melody caught on and asked, "You want me to steer you?"

Hunter affirmed with a grunt.

"Okay," Melody gripped the handles tighter. She tilted to the right, and Hunter turned right. She tilted harder to the left, and Hunter turned a sharper left. Melody smiled and said, "All right, let's go back to the water."

Hunter, guided by Melody, flew back to the coastline. He dove down the cliff and between two towering rock spires before beginning to skim the water.

Now, finally, Melody was laughing. She felt free at last.

There was a fishing ship some distance off the coast, and Melody decided to fly in for a closer look. She steered Hunter toward it, keeping low and close to the water. Then, as they were mere seconds from crashing into the hull, she let loose a "Woohoo!" and pulled up on the handles, causing Hunter to curve upward. The surprised crew was buffeted with a gust of wind and a spray of seawater as they went.

"Keep going up!" Melody shouted, keeping Hunter on his current course. When they had flown up high, she steered Hunter back around to behold her kingdom. She could see the beautiful, wooded coastline, jagged in every area except for one place far to the right. It was Carnelian Cove, surrounded on every side by tall, smooth, green mountains.

"Wow," Melody breathed.

"Finally enjoying yourself, I see!" Eli called from below.

"Yeah," Melody replied with a blush.

"What do you say we take a closer look at the cove?"

Melody smiled. "I would love to!"

"All right! Let's go!"

Eli, Kaya, Melody, and Hunter flew to Carnelian Cove. They skirted the mountains and dove down the forested cliffs sheltering the bay, all the while staying far enough from the city to avoid attracting unwanted attention. They rested for a while at the top of the highest mountain, and then they were off again.

Over the next few hours, Eli did not disappoint in his assignment to show Melody around the kingdom of Rhema. There wasn't a single part of the island kingdom they didn't fly through. Melody grew confident in her ability to ride a dragon. More importantly, she became more comfortable with Eli's guidance and leadership. The adventure led Melody to become very fond of Eli, even to the point where her fondness outweighed her skepticism.

Despite her progress, Eli knew she still had her doubts. For the last leg of their tour of Rhema, he knew exactly where to take her.

"Mel," Eli said, eyes glimmering, "there's one last place I want you to see."

They were now reclining in a grassy field near a west-facing cliff. The ocean foamed far below, sparkling blue and silver against the molten sky, which was fiery with the coming of sunset. Hunter and Kaya drank heartily from a stream nearby.

Melody looked at Eli and asked, "What do you mean? I thought we've seen everything already. Besides, wouldn't you say it's getting late?"

"I saved this one for last because it's very special to me. It's an ocean cave not far from here. It can only be accessed during low tides, and this is the perfect hour to go."

"All right," Melody replied, standing up. "Let's go, then."

The two of them mounted their dragons and took off. Eli led the way down to the ocean and skimmed the edge of the cliff for a short distance before he had Kaya hover in place.

Hunter hovered beside Kaya as their riders beheld the cave. It was a yawning, black void with dark blue water pulling in and out. It echoed in the most ominous manner.

"*That* cave?" Melody asked.

"Yup, that's the one. Now, we'll have to trust our dragons to guide us through. They have good night vision, so they'll know where to go."

"I thought you wanted me to see something in there. How will I see anything if it's dark?"

"You'll see." Eli winked. Then he nudged Kaya and said, "To the back of the cave."

Kaya disappeared into the yawning cavern.

"You too, Hunter," Melody told her dragon, and Hunter flew inside.

To Melody, it seemed like they were flying for several minutes through the pitch-dark blackness. She could tell the cave was narrowing by the sound of the dragons' wingbeats echoing off the walls, and by the sound of the stirring water below. Melody stayed low against Hunter's back, fearful she would hit her head on the ceiling of the cave.

Suddenly, there was a splash as Hunter landed in the water. Melody yelped in surprise, thinking Hunter was going to sink and take her along with him.

Eli's voice called from just ahead, "It's all right, Mel! The water's shallow enough here for the dragons to walk. Kaya, how about some light?"

A second later, thanks to a steady flame in Kaya's mouth, Melody was able to see her surroundings. The cave in front of them was too narrow for the dragons to fly through, but since the water was shallow, they could walk perfectly well through the tunnel. The water looked to be about four feet deep.

"This is why we need a low tide," Eli explained as Kaya and Hunter ventured deeper into the cave. "Otherwise, this part of the cave would be submerged."

"Have you been here before?" Melody asked.

"No. Only one person has come here."

"Do you know him? Or her?"

"I did."

"Oh. Is he or she dead?"

"Yes, he's dead."

"High tide?" Melody guessed.

"No."

"Oh." Melody looked at Eli, whose countenance had fallen. "Were you close friends?"

"Yes."

Soon, they emerged into a massive, cavernous space. The floor sloped upward, so the dragons surfaced onto packed, sandy ground. High on the vaulted ceiling, in addition to the many stalactites, there were small crevices through which weak shafts of light came down in rays. The cave was so large, Kaya's fire couldn't allow them to see to the other side.

"This is it," Eli said, sliding off Kaya and landing with a thud on the sandy ground.

"A dark, empty cave?"

"Not quite." Eli pointed into the darkness ahead. "Ignite the basin."

Kaya squawked and launched a fireball into the darkness. It careened through empty space for a second before hitting a stone basin carved into the wall of the cave. The projectile burst with a unique display of orange and blue sparks. The basin filled with liquid blue fire, which spread rapidly down small troughs extending along the base of the wall. The cavern brightened to acquire a mystical, shimmering blue glow.

Several troughs on the right side of the room extended up the wall and ran along the ceiling. The blue fire in these troughs illuminated a peculiar pattern at the back of the cave.

Melody squinted her eyes at the pattern as it came to light. She gasped in surprise. "It's…it's a mural! A *huge* mural!"

"Go on, take a closer look!"

She slid off Hunter and ran toward it. Eli, Hunter, and Kaya followed close behind.

Melody stood in front of the mural, awestruck by the enormous piece of art before her. "Eli, I've never seen anything like it! Your friend was a true artist, and in a cave, no less!"

"Indeed," Eli agreed. "What do you see?"

"Hmm," Melody studied the mural. There were many things going on, so she began with the focal point in the very center. "There's a man in the center…no, an elf. A grand, wise-looking elf, and he's sitting on a throne. The Great King," Melody said, looking at Eli for confirmation. Then she continued, "On either side of him are two more thrones. On the right is..." she trailed off.

"Who?" Eli pressed. "Who is it?"

Melody stepped closer to the mural. She was three feet away from it now, staring up at the dazzling figure sitting on the right throne. "It's me."

"That's right."

"I-it's the most beautiful painting of me I've ever seen."

Even as she was still processing, her eyes drifted to the throne on the left. When she realized who was sitting there, she held her breath. "It...it can't be, can it?" She looked at Eli, her eyes demanding an explanation.

"What do you see?" Eli asked.

"I know what I see, but I...I can't believe..." Melody looked again at the figure on the throne. "Eli, it's you. But, it's *you* you. *Human* you, just like you are right now. A bit shinier perhaps, but still *you*."

"Yes," Eli said, standing next to Melody. "What else do you see?"

Melody was overwhelmed, but she continued to examine other parts of the mural. "Well, surrounding the thrones, there are four creatures. Titans, right? One is like a wheel of fire, the second is like a whirling thunderstorm, the third is like an erupting volcano, and the fourth is like a breaching wave. All around them are groups of shiny elves playing instruments. Galyyrim, I think. And below it all, there's the realm. The sea, the land, the trees, the clouds, even cities," Melody walked up to place her finger on a painted city. After a moment, she turned to face Eli. "Who did this?"

"His name was Uriah. Do you remember him?"

Melody shook her head.

"You killed him."

Melody's jaw dropped. "W-what do you mean I killed him?"

"Do you remember what he told you before he was executed?"

Melody became flustered. "Wait just a minute! You're talking about those Seers, aren't you?"

"Yes," Eli said, his eyes filled with sorrow. "He was a zealous, passionate follower of the Great King. A wonderful fellow. He fled from your officials when his actions caused them to seek his life. The Great King showed him to this place, where he spent twenty years in hiding. During that time, he painted this mural so the mysteries revealed to him would be saved for future generations. Then, the Great King led him to confront you one last time, and he was killed."

Melody wanted to unleash a violent rant upon Eli about how much she loathed Seers, but her heart stopped her. The part of her that loved Eli and everything he stood for came alongside her frustrated ego and sang it a lullaby, like taming a dragon. Then she remembered Uriah and what he said: "Your father, the King, remembers you, and he loves you! The Prince of the Sea is coming soon, and he will deliver you from the power of the Serpent once and for all! Remember the Great King and follow his ways! He doesn't want you to continue in your suffering, but to return to Marindel as the bride of the Great Prince!"

As Uriah's words cycled through her head, Melody looked again at the thrones in the center. The painting of her was the most stunning portrayal of herself that she had ever seen. The painting of Eli was likewise staggering to behold. He was handsome and regal, yes, but he looked *exactly* like the Eli who was in the cave with her now: in appearance, simply an ordinary man.

Everything began to make sense.

The Great King gave Uriah such extraordinary wisdom, he was able to paint this intricate mural down to the detail on Eli's face.

Uriah lived two centuries ago, but somehow, he knew.

He knew Eli was coming.

More than that, Uriah knew Eli was coming as an ordinary man.

Bringing it to a crescendo, Uriah knew Eli was coming as an ordinary man to court Melody and take her back to Marindel and marry her, making her a Princess of the Sea once again and a legitimate daughter of the Great King.

This is what he was trying to tell her all along, he and all the Seers before him. And she had them all killed for it. Her eyes welled up with tears. "What have I done?"

Eli came alongside Melody and took her hand. She immediately hugged him tight and began to sob. "I'm sorry, I'm *so* sorry!"

"Don't worry, Mel," Eli said softly, "I forgive you."

"I deserve to die," Melody mumbled.

"No. You are forgiven."

Melody continued to weep as her thoughts and emotions shifted. Inner walls came down, doubts were washed away, and lies were cut down. The iron hold the Serpent kept on her soul for so long finally began to lose its grip. Finally, at long last, she spoke.

"I believe."

"What's that?" Eli asked, pulling out of the embrace to see her face.

"I believe," she repeated, meeting his gaze. "You are Eli, the Great Prince of the Sea. The Son of the Great King."

Eli smiled and hugged her again, he himself now beginning to weep. "At last, you're beginning to understand!" He chuckled, resting his head against hers. "The Great King has revealed this to you, and you must treasure it with all your heart. Do not let this seed of belief be taken from you. By it, you will be saved, and I will take you to Marindel with me to live with our father, the Great King, forever."

It was late at night when Eli and Melody returned to Diamond City. They flew Kaya and Hunter up to the balcony of Melody's room and had them perch along the banister. There, Melody dismounted and said goodbye to Eli.

"When will I see you again?" Melody asked, looking up at him.

"Meet me tomorrow, at noon, in the marketplace by the textile shop." His eyes glimmered. "We'll have a great time!"

"I can't wait," Melody replied, returning his loving gaze.

"Goodnight, Mel. I love you."

"Goodnight."

Eli looked at her a moment longer before nudging Kaya to push off the balcony and glide into the starry night, back to Caruso's manor where the dragons belonged.

Hunter crawled onto the balcony to give Melody an affectionate nudge before he jumped after Kaya.

Melody watched them go until she could see them no longer. She sighed deeply, smiling as she recounted the exciting events of the day.

That man is something else, she thought. *He doesn't just know about me. He knows me. He sees me, as I am, right now. Every thought. Every feeling. I'm an irredeemable mess, desperate for affection, yet unable to really earn it. But still, he wants me. He enjoys me. Today, Eli's piercing words and penetrating gaze tore down my facade, leaving me vulnerable before him. I should have been terrified. But, never before have I felt so…* safe. *He is so gentle, and so kind! His presence is like a shield, protecting me from every outside threat. When I'm with him, I feel like I can do anything. I rode a* dragon *today, for crying out loud! Who can this man be, if not the Prince of Marindel? Oh, I can't wait to see Eli again! I'd better get some rest before our next adventure!*

Giddy and beaming, Melody walked into her room. It was dark inside, so she went to light the oil lamp on her nightstand. When she did, she yelped at the sight of a person sitting on a chair in the corner. She didn't grow any less tense when she realized it was one of her officials, the elder with the white beard.

"Where were you today?" he asked.

"Visiting other villages in the kingdom. Why? Did you miss me?"

"What were you doing in those villages?"

"Having fun. You know, queen stuff."

"What came over you that caused you to traipse around Rhema without your wise council to escort you?"

"I needed a break. You guys don't give me much space, you know."

"But you *weren't* alone, were you?"

By his tone, Melody supposed he already knew the answer, so there was no reason to deny the obvious. "Nope, I was with my new friend, Eli. You know, the Prince of Marindel? He's actually really great."

"Have you gone mad?" The elder stood. "That man is no prince! He's a troublemaker! A peasant who's had too much wine to drink!"

Melody laughed. "Yeah, he gets that a lot. Someone called him a sorcerer today. That's a new one, huh?"

"Milady, this is serious! We've been receiving complaints about him from all over the kingdom. He's meddling in everyone's affairs, performing magic tricks, and fostering division between us and the Tethysians. And let's not even mention the whole Prince of Marindel nonsense."

"Oh, loosen up. You just have to get to know him, that's all."

"Rubbish," the elder spat. "Listen carefully. I don't want to see or hear of you spending time with that man ever again. Do you understand?"

"No."

"Then you'd better take tonight to think about it," the elder said, wagging his finger. "If this continues, there *will* be consequences. As your appointed officials, we cannot allow any threat to the peace and security of Rhema. You ought to tell him to leave, and leave quickly."

"All right. Shall I go with him?"

"And abandon your people and the entire kingdom? That's absurd! You're not going anywhere!"

"Well, what if I marry him and become a queen of Marindel? Rhema will become a state of Marindel, and then we won't have to negotiate with Tethysians anymore. We could fight them and win."

"Milady, listen to me!" The elder stepped closer and enunciated his words very clearly. "He is *not* the Prince of Marindel!"

"Yes, he is!" Melody enunciated with equal clarity.

The elder pointed his finger at Melody's face and glared at her. "One more chance. Just one. If we see or hear of you participating in his ridiculous antics again, you will be placed under house arrest. *He*, on the other hand, will be dealt with as we see fit."

"Challenge accepted."

"Hmph." The elder turned to leave, saying more politely as he went, "Good night, Milady."

After the elder shut the door, Melody thought about the tense conversation. Despite her initial resolve, she knew his threats were legitimate. He would stop at nothing to make sure Eli ended up with the same fate as all the Seers before him.

But this time, it would be different.

They can't arrest him if I don't let them, Melody reasoned. *I'm the Queen of Rhema, and they ultimately have to do what I say. If they disobey me, they'll be guilty of treason, and I can convince the Tethysians to back me up on that. Not that I'll be needing them, though. Eli is clever enough to avoid my officials already, but I'll have to warn him tomorrow when I see him.*

With those thoughts, Melody prepared herself for bed and went to sleep with eager anticipation for the day ahead.

Over the next few days, Melody continued to spend time with Eli. She warned him of her officials' hatred toward him, but that didn't stop Eli from being himself. That is, from spending time with the people of Rhema, serving them in practical everyday matters, healing diseases and injuries, telling stories about Marindel, and teaching values of justice, humility, and love for one another.

As Melody accompanied Eli on these adventures, she discovered the sole motivating force behind everything he did was a genuine love and respect for all people. The more Melody spent time with Eli, the more his loving spirit began to take hold of her as well. Melody found herself seeing people more favorably. Much to her surprise, she became more willing to talk and spend time with them.

One afternoon, Eli and Melody visited Jasper Village to have lunch with the family they encountered before: Trisha, her husband Auben, the little boy Trevor, and his older sister Lia. The family was amazed at how open and friendly Melody had become. And of course, they reckoned Eli was the reason behind the change. Melody thought the afternoon was very pleasant, and upon departing, she wondered aloud, "Why did I refuse to spend time with them on our first visit here?"

Eli said, "Don't worry, Mel, I knew your heart wasn't in the right place yet. Today was the perfect time for it. Besides, if we had stayed with them, we wouldn't have gotten to ride dragons." He gave her a playful wink.

During this time, Eli and Melody had many close calls with the Rheman officials and the Tethysian soldiers. Both groups were becoming more suspicious of Eli's strange activity and they were afraid he and Melody were spending far too much time together.

Melody's officials, under ordinary circumstances, were well respected by the common people of Rhema. However, it was an unspoken truth that they cared little for the people, and Eli was bringing that truth to light. As a result, the people favored Eli with growing resolve. This effect multiplied when Melody sided with Eli instead of her officials, thereby stripping them of their legitimacy before the people.

In addition, though the officials tried to place Melody under house arrest, she wielded her authority as the Queen of Rhema to go wherever she pleased. They knew very well how stubborn she could be, though they'd never experienced her attitude working against them before. This was something they sorely resented.

As for the Tethysians, many of them weren't concerned with Eli's good deeds and bouts with the officials as much as they were with his statements about the Great King, and his "sorcerous" actions. The Tethysian Empire as a whole, having conquered half of the realm by 104 IE, had many experiences dealing with sorcerers and political instigators. The two qualities combined in one person, one who also had favor with the common people, was a triple threat in the Empire's eyes. Nevertheless, despite the incredible zeal of some officers like Matthias, they were unable to muster enough support for a successful attempt at capturing Eli. The Tethysian governor, specifically, had no interest in giving a mandate to catch a charity worker.

However, despite these things, the Great Serpent was closing in on his illustrious target, knowing exactly what to do to tilt events in his favor.

And he would not relent, not even for a second.

Comprehension

1) List two similarities and two differences between the dragon-flight scene and the flooded palace scene.

2) Describe the symbolic meaning of the cavern mural.

3) What claim does Melody make about Eli's identity?

4) Why do the Rheman officials feel threatened by Eli? How about the Tethysians?

Reflection

1) In the Old Testament, many characters and events foretold the coming of the Messiah. References to Jesus can be found in almost every book of the Bible! Which prophecies are most significant or memorable to you, and why? If you can't think of any, look up "Old Testament prophecies about Jesus" and write down three Scriptures that stand out to you.

8

The Prince of Love
Summer, 104 IE

Melody was standing with Eli on a cloud high in the sky. He took her by the shoulders with a grand smile and said, "Melody, I want you to jump. Can you do that for me?"

Melody shook her head. "That'd be insane!"

"Come on, Mel! Trust me!"

She thought for a moment and then shrugged. "Well, all right. But you'd better protect me!"

"I will. Don't worry," Eli said, grasping her hands tightly.

"Here I go!" Melody jumped off the cloud. She fell for what seemed like an eternity. The sprawling Rhema countryside was below, glistening in the noonday sun. It was so beautiful, Melody forgot she was falling.

Her eyes locked onto a small gray speck on the landscape below. When she did so, suddenly, the speck grew into an enormous metal dragon's head, mouth gaping wide and filled with sword-like teeth.

With a surge of panic, Melody screamed and flailed about as the dragon's jaws closed over her like a steel trap.

Melody awoke with a horrified shout. Breathing hard, she took in the safe and familiar surroundings of her room.

It was just a dream. An utterly terrifying dream.

Even knowing that, Melody's heart was hurt. She put her trust in Eli, and in the end, it resulted in her death. Didn't Eli know there was a giant metal dragon head down there waiting for her? How could he tell her to jump like that? Eli would never do such a thing!

Or would he? The thought entered Melody's mind. It was the Serpent speaking, but he used a voice resembling Melody's own. *It will only take one mistake, one moment of misplaced trust, to end up in the jaws of death.*

Melody sat on her bed with her arms wrapped around her knees, pondering this terrifying revelation. Eli had proven to be trustworthy thus far. But, what if, just one time…?

You cannot place your trust in others, the Serpent spoke within her. *If, when you place your trust in Eli, he turns and stabs you in the back, you have only yourself to blame. Only you can protect yourself.*

Melody shook her head and banished the thought. *How crazy. Eli would never do such a thing. He never would! It's not like him. He loves me. I know he does.*

Then you'd better not fail him and change his mind.

"Rubbish," Melody said aloud. "I can't believe I'm thinking like this. Eli has loved me since we were kids. He's been waiting all this time to see me again, and now he's finally here. After all the wrong I've already done, I can't do anything to make him change his mind. He knows me completely, and he loves me unconditionally."

We shall see, the Serpent said, and left Melody to her own thoughts.

After calming down, Melody went to sleep again. The next day, she met Eli in the apple orchard and spent time with him as usual. She didn't act any different, but deep down, she couldn't forget the imagery of her dream and the terror it struck in her inmost being.

Throughout the next two weeks, Melody had many similar dreams.

One night, she dreamt that Eli had stopped to help a young woman with a hunched back. He healed her back so she could stand up perfectly straight, and the girl became inexplicably beautiful. Thereafter, Eli returned every day to visit her. When Melody questioned him about it, he said, "Melody, I've decided I love her more than I love you."

Using that dream, the Serpent planted envy in Melody's heart. From that night on, as Eli continued visiting villages and helping people, Melody became jealous whenever Eli gave others more attention than her, even if just for a moment. But she never said anything about it because she didn't want to appear selfish.

The more these dreams came, the more Melody began to doubt Eli's character and her worthiness in his eyes. Outwardly, she still followed him, but she didn't tell him or anyone else about her doubts because she didn't want to be thought of as incompetent or weak for doubting him even after everything they'd been through.

This, of course, was all the work of the Serpent as he manipulated her thoughts and exploited her past wounds to cast doubt on what she thought she believed was true.

One evening, Eli took Melody to the apple orchard. Though they had spent many hours in the orchard before, this was their first visit after sundown.

"How are you feeling?" Eli asked as they walked through the trees.

"I'm well," Melody replied, looking up at the dark branches against the twilit sky.

"Is that so?"

"Mhmm."

"You've been quieter the past few days. What's on your mind?" Though Eli already knew of Melody's doubts, he wanted her to admit she had them. Otherwise, her heart wouldn't be open to his encouragement and affirmation.

Melody couldn't discern Eli's intentions, so she kept her thoughts to herself. "Nothing really. I mean, all of this is still new to me. I'm still…taking it all in, you know?"

"I see. Well, tonight, I have a surprise for you."

"Really?" Melody asked, her interest piquing.

"Yes," Eli replied, his face glowing. "You've never ventured around the countryside at night before, have you?"

"Nope. It's too dark, too scary."

"Perhaps. But I'll be your guide tonight, so you have nothing to fear."

Melody smiled. "All right, if you say so." She had a tiny prick of doubt even as she spoke, but she repressed it.

"Great," Eli grinned and began to run. "Come on, follow me!"

"Wait, where are we going?" Melody called as she went after him.

"You'll see!"

They ran between two hills laden with apple trees, then took a right and ran up another hill and down the other side, zigzagging around boulders and tree trunks the whole way. It wasn't long before Melody was panting for breath. It was also very dark, and she was afraid she'd trip.

"Come along! Just a little further!" Eli called. "Don't lose sight of me!"

Melody was becoming frustrated with Eli for leading her on through a gloomy forest. Though she was getting exhausted and longed for a place to rest, she kept her gaze on him. It was strange; Eli seemed to be brighter than anything else she could see, almost as if he were glowing. When she looked at him, she could run effortlessly without any worry. But when she looked away, at the rough terrain below her feet or the dark forms of trees and boulders all around, she became frightened and exhausted. Even then, all she had to do was look again at Prince Eli, and she found her strength quickly renewed. It didn't take Melody long to realize this, so she remained focused on Eli for the remainder of the journey.

Eli stopped.

Melody skidded to a halt behind him, gasping for breath. They were now standing on the rim of a large pond, the waters of which were still and reflected the starry night above.

"Shhh," Eli whispered, "Look, over there."

Melody followed Eli's gaze. There, on the other side of the pond, was a majestic unicorn, shimmering in the starlight, and feeding on the apples hanging from a tree.

"Beautiful, isn't it?" Eli whispered. "We have a perfect view! I don't think she's noticed us yet."

Melody stayed silent. Deep down, she greatly resented unicorns. Every time she had an encounter with one, it tried to attack her. She and her officials considered unicorns to be pests because they roamed about freely, trespassing into farmers' fields, eating their fill, and trampling whatever remained.

"Have you ever petted a unicorn, Mel?"

Melody shook her head.

"Oh, they're *so* soft! Let's get a closer look. How about it?"

Melody hesitated. She didn't want to refuse him, but she also didn't want to get any closer to the unicorn. She searched for an excuse. "I-I'm not sure it's possible to get over there. See, the pond is in the way, and there's thick underbrush growing all along the edge. The unicorn will hear us coming and run away long before we can touch it."

"We can make it across that pond easily. Do you trust me?"

"Uh…" Melody wasn't sure what he was asking her to trust him to do. Crossing the pond would be unpleasant, muddy, and cold.

"Do you trust me?" he repeated.

She wanted to. Despite her doubts, she was still incredibly fond of Eli. He had never let her down before, at least not in the waking realm. Remembering his love for her and drawing strength from her seedling of love for him, she mustered all the courage she had to say, "Yes. I trust you."

Eli smiled and reached forward. "Here, take my hand."

Melody took his hand, blushing as she looked into his eyes.

"Now, just look at the unicorn," Eli said, pointing at it. "How marvelous! Do you know much about unicorns?"

"No, not really. I've never liked them much, and they don't like me, either."

"I understand. Let me tell you something about unicorns, Mel. They're far more perceptive than horses, or even dragons! A unicorn can see the intentions of a person's heart; whether they're good or evil. They will react accordingly to what they see in your heart."

Melody whispered sharply, "What are you trying to say?"

"I'm saying you've changed for the better. I've seen the ways you've grown as we've spent time together. Your spirit has become gentle and loving. Every passing day, I see more of the innocent little girl I once knew, perfected in all the beauty my father saw in you from the very beginning. You've endured a very painful life on the surface, and you've made many unwise and selfish choices. But, Mel, *all* of it can be redeemed. From the ashes of your soul can come a beautiful vine more fruitful than it was at first, before the release of the Serpent. That is what I've come to show you."

Melody listened, her gaze fixed on the unicorn. On an intellectual level, she had no idea what Eli meant, but her spirit leapt and grabbed at every word. She felt understood by him. More than that, she felt loved and appreciated, despite her dark past and her present rebellious nature.

She looked at Eli to say something, but when she did, she realized they were standing atop the surface of the pond, a dozen feet from the shore.

"Eli! Wh-what!?" Melody clung to Eli.

"Melody, it's all right! Don't be surprised to find yourself doing impossible things when you put your trust in me and the Great King. Remember when we ran through the orchard earlier? As you fixed your eyes on me, you didn't need to worry about what path to take or whether or not your feet would slip. It works the same in every matter of life. It has pleased the Great King tonight to allow us to walk upon this pond so you may know even more what it's like to trust me."

"Whoa." Melody slowly let go of Eli and stood freely upon the surface. Their footsteps hardly rippled the pond at all, but the water around their feet glowed with beautiful hues of dancing blue.

"Look," Eli pointed at the unicorn, which had noticed them when their voices raised. It stood still, watching curiously with its ears perked and its tail swishing back and forth.

Melody cowered at the sight of it. "You're not still wanting to touch it, are you?"

"I have a better idea," Eli said, cracking an adventurous grin.

"How about we ride it?"

Melody's eyes widened. "What's with you and riding things!? Why in the kingdom of Rhema would I want to ride a wild unicorn!?"

Even as she spoke, Eli began walking across the pond toward the unicorn.

The unicorn leaned forward and wiggled its nose to take in Eli's scent. Then it trotted several steps into the pond to meet him, ears flicking happily.

Once they met, Eli brushed the unicorn's snout with his hand and said, "Hey there, wanna go for a run tonight? Stretch your big, strong legs?"

The unicorn whinnied and nudged Eli's face with its nose.

Eli chuckled, and he called, "Come on, Mel! There's nothing to fear."

"But...didn't you say it sees my heart? What if it doesn't like me? I told you unicorns don't like me."

"What else did I tell you?"

Melody knew what Eli wanted her to say, but she was still fighting her dislike of unicorns.

While she delayed, Eli slung himself onto the unicorn's back. He looked at Melody with excitement in his gaze and stretched out his hand. "Come with me!"

"But, Eli..." Melody trailed off as she looked at him. She was captivated by his eyes, the way his hair glistened in the starlight, the way he smiled at her and sat upon the unicorn's back, calling her to join him. Eli *wanted* her to join him. She couldn't help but blush, and she threw her hesitation aside. "All right, all right. Only because you're with me." She took his hand.

Eli pulled Melody up onto the unicorn's back, and she sat behind him.

The unicorn snorted and flicked its ears, adjusting its stance to accommodate the weight on its back. But it didn't seem at all frustrated with Melody.

"Hold on tight," Eli said over his shoulder. "Are you ready?"

Melody wrapped her arms around Eli's waist. "Yeah."

Eli spurred the unicorn on. It whinnied and set off at a gallop, sending up a spray of water as it moved out of the pond and into the darkness of the orchard.

At first, Melody was dismayed that they were once again traveling through the trees, but her disappointment didn't last long. A moment later, they emerged from the orchard and galloped into the rolling, starlit grasslands of Rhema. They were heading east, in a perfect position to witness the rising full moon. A cool breeze blew over the tall grass, bending it in gentle waves. Flashing pinpricks of light shimmered across the countryside; hundreds of fireflies in every direction. As Eli and Melody rode forth, the insects skittered before them like wind-blown sparks.

Eli directed the unicorn with skill and expertise. Whether it was dodging a boulder here or jumping a pond there, he did so with a calm trust in the unicorn's ability to overcome every obstacle. He never reprimanded the animal, but nudged and spoke simple words to guide it on its way. As a result of Eli's expert riding, Melody was able to forget her dislike of unicorns and take in the experience. It happened quicker on this night than on the day they flew dragons.

Melody relished the nighttime air, the enchanting chorus of crickets and frogs, and the sparkling lights dancing to the rhythm of the unicorn's hoofbeats. But, however impressed she was by this mesmerizing dreamworld, she was most fascinated by the man sitting in front of her. The only man who had ever *truly* loved her, wanted her, and protected her.

"Eli," she said after a few moments, "This is truly wonderful."

Eli turned back to smile at her. "I knew you would enjoy it, Mel."

"I mean it," Melody insisted, wrapping her arms tighter around him. "I'm really happy to be here with you tonight."

Eli's face brightened even more. "And I'm glad to be with you, my beloved."

For another half an hour, Eli and Melody rode the unicorn throughout the moonlit countryside. They hardly spoke a word. But for once, it wasn't because Melody was lost in thought. She was enjoying the present moment with Eli, whom she loved, and all she could think about was how much she loved him and couldn't wait to marry him. She had never met another man like Eli, who cared for her and pursued her like she was the most precious treasure in the realm.

Eli brought the unicorn to a stop at the summit of a high hill upon which stood a massive camphor tree. The gnarled trunk and branches of the tree towered above everything else in the grassland, and its luscious green canopy was dense like a cloud. From the foot of the tree, with the help of the moonlight, Eli and Melody could see endlessly in every direction: the firefly-speckled fields, a few trees here and there, dark forested areas further on the horizon, and from whence they came, the faraway dimly-lit stone edifice that was Diamond City.

Eli hopped down from the unicorn's back and helped Melody down as well. Then he said to the unicorn, "Thank you, friend. Go frolic as you please."

The unicorn whinnied, shaking its silky mane, and trotted away into the night.

Melody looked around, her gaze lingering on the tree nearby. "What is this place?"

"It's one of my favorite spots in all of Rhema," Eli said, his voice reverent.

She looked around again but saw nothing interesting. "Why?"

"This is a place where the presence of my father, the Great King, dwells strongly. I come here almost every night to commune with him. He gives me strength, confidence, focus, and direction."

"It's quite far from the city."

"Yes. I prefer to seek my father in solitude, where I can devote myself to hearing his voice."

"Is that why you never sleep in the city?"

"Yes. But tonight, I would like to share this moment with you."

"Oh? What kind of moment?" Melody asked, stepping closer to him.

"This intimacy I have with my father," Eli said, taking Melody by the hand, "is something I would like to pass on to you."

"That's...great," Melody replied, not understanding what he meant. "How?"

"Do you remember the gift he gave you back in Marindel? The royal power and authority sealed within the amulet?"

"A little bit, maybe." She didn't want to remember. It was because of the amulet that the Serpent was released. With its power, the Serpent was able to cause unmitigated death and destruction. Melody didn't want to have that power again. *I don't deserve it,* she thought.

"In the near future," Eli said, "the power and authority bestowed by the Great King as an inheritance will not be confined to any particular amulet, nor will it be set apart for one person. It will dwell in the hearts of all who choose to follow the Great King. These he will, like you, adopt to become his sons and daughters. In that way, the Kingdom of Marindel will triumph over the Serpent and his dark forces once and for all."

"Wait, so..." Melody was confused.

"I know it's hard to understand now," Eli said, poking Melody on the nose. "But keep it in mind for another time."

"Why are you telling me this if you know I'm not going to understand it?"

"Because I'm confident you will *someday,*" Eli said with a gentle smile. "I believe you will."

"Okay." Melody blushed.

"Now, you've seen the things I've done here in Rhema. You've heard my words, and you've seen the power of the Great King released through my actions."

"Mhmm." Melody stared into his eyes. "There has never been another man like you, and I don't believe there ever will be."

"I've done these things to set an example for you and for those who will soon believe. I have no power of my own, but because I watch and listen for the nudges of my father the King, and I do what he says, he lends me his strength to do the impossible. You've experienced it as well; have you noticed? When you sing unto the Great King, the power of life flows around you and causes plants to grow and bloom."

Melody thought back to when she tamed Hunter and Kaya and how the grass around her had bloomed and scorched grass was healed. She nodded. "Yeah, I did notice that."

"This is what I've been trying to show you. The Great King's power is available to you, just as it is to me, when you listen for his voice and step out to do what he says. Do you remember, long ago, when you set out to find this land? The Great King led you here because you listened to him. Since then, you and your people have forgotten the Great King and have governed according to your own wisdom. The consequences of your actions have become evident. However, the Great King doesn't want you to be destroyed by the cunning schemes of the Serpent, who is currently the tyrant of this realm. The King created a way for you, and soon, for all sentient beings, to escape from the control of the Serpent and enter into the Kingdom of Marindel."

"And that way is you," Melody said, wrapping her arms around his shoulders. "Isn't it?"

"Indeed," Eli said, embracing her. "It is."

"Oh, can we be married already?" Melody asked with a longing sigh, resting her forehead against his. "Take me away from this place, from all the horrors of politics and people-pleasing, and the death and destruction that follows me everywhere I go. Take me to Marindel, where I can be beside you forever."

Eli held her close, looking deeply into her eyes. "Do you know that I love you, Mel?"

"Yes. I know you love me very much."

"Do you know I will never stop loving you, no matter what happens?"

"Yes," Melody said, placing her hand on Eli's head and stroking his hair. "No matter what comes our way, your love will endure forever."

Eli smiled. A single tear rolled down his cheek.

"You're…crying? What's wrong?"

Eli's expression evolved into a mixture of joy and grief. "If only it was *that* simple."

"What do you mean?"

For a moment, Eli appeared to have an inward battle in his mind. He glanced at the ground while several tears streamed down his face. He said, almost inaudibly, "Father, I trust you." Then he looked at Melody and said, "No matter what happens, Mel—no matter *what* happens—remember I love you. You *must* remember, I love you."

Before she could reply, Eli moved in to kiss her. Melody surrendered, holding him tight and returning the kiss with passion.

After a few seconds, they separated and stared into each other's eyes again. Melody's gaze was giddy and bright with adoration. Eli's gaze was strong and loving, gentle and wise—yet, there were undertones of sorrow.

"You look like you need another kiss, mister," Melody said with a grin.

Eli stepped out of her embrace and took her hands, holding them tight. "Mel, there's something I must tell you."

"Yeah?"

"I will not be here for much longer. Soon, I must return to Marindel."

"Oh…" Melody took a moment to ponder before replying, "Well, this is great news! I'm so excited to go back to Marindel with you to be married! Then Rhema will be your kingdom, and Marindel will be mine. Together, we can resist the Empire and every enemy who comes against us. And we can live happily ever after."

Eli didn't respond the way Melody thought he would. She thought he'd be joyful and confident, but instead, Eli was troubled. He sighed deeply and looked at the ground.

"Eli, what's wrong?"

"Mel," Eli said, looking deep into her eyes. "We *will* be married. I promise, one day I will be fully yours, and you will be fully mine. You will take your rightful place as the Princess of the Sea at the right hand of our father, the Great King. But first…"

"First…?" Melody whispered, willing him to continue.

"I must return to Marindel alone. Where I am going, you cannot come. Not yet."

Melody's eyes widened. She couldn't believe what she was hearing. "What do you mean? You're going to…*leave* me?"

"No. Though you may not see me for a while, you must remember I will never abandon you. I will never stop loving you, and I will always, *always* remember you. Just as I came for you this time, I will come again when the time is right. But many things must take place before then."

Melody was distraught. "B-but why? *Why* can't I come with you?"

"It's too much to explain now. One day, you'll understand."

"But I want to understand *now!*"

"Shh," Eli said, brushing her cheek with his hand. "Just remember, Mel. Always remember, I love you. Never forget, no matter what. Can you do that for me?"

Melody fumbled for words, her lip quivering. "I, uh…yes. Yes. I think so."

Eli smiled and nodded. He stooped down to pick up a fallen berry from the camphor tree, picked out the seed, and dug a small place for it in the ground. After burying it, he stood and looked at Melody with endearment as another tear rolled down his cheek. "Then let us trust the Great King together. His plan is wonderful, his ways are good, and his leadership is wise."

The Great Story of Marindel

Comprehension

1) Explain how the Serpent uses nightmares to weaken Melody's trust in Eli.

2) What enables Melody to run through the twilit forest without any exhaustion or fear?

3) Why does Eli regularly spend the night at the giant camphor tree?

4) According to Eli, to whom will the Great King soon grant his royal inheritance, and in what form?

5) Why does Eli begin to weep? How does Melody interpret his response?

6) What is the significance of Eli planting a camphor seed? Refer to John 12:24.

Reflection

1) Read John 14:1-6 and John 16:16-22. Imagine yourself in the place of Jesus, knowing you would be arrested and tried that very night. How would it feel to tell your best friends that you would soon be going away? How would it feel to see and hear their responses?

9

The Prince of Sorrow
Summer, 104 IE

Melody jerked awake with a gasp for breath, her heart pounding relentlessly.

Another nightmare.

It had been two nights since she last saw Eli, and on both nights, she was plagued with terrible dreams. In every case, unbeknownst to Melody, the Great Serpent had been working to disrupt the very foundation of her trust in Eli. Though she still loved Eli and longed to see him, the knowledge that he would soon be leaving without her was too much to bear.

Now, on this night, the stage was set for the Serpent's plan to be launched in full.

"Mel!" she heard a distant call.

She quieted her breath and listened. "Eli?"

"Mel, where are you?" the voice called again.

Recognizing his voice, a surge of joy overtook her. She cloaked herself in a night robe and hurried onto the balcony. She looked over the banister and called, "Eli, I'm here!"

No answer.

Melody looked, but she saw no one. "Eli?"

"Over here!" The voice came from inside the palace.

She went back across her room and opened the door to peer down the hallway. It was dark and eerie, with the waning moon casting pale white light through the windows on the vaulted ceiling. With a nervous frown, Melody ventured down the hallway. She was careful to ensure her bare feet made no noise on the marble floor, lest she wake her officials or alert the guards.

"Come, this way," the voice called ahead of her.

She followed the voice, passing through several halls and rooms as she went. Oddly, she noticed the voice never seemed to grow louder or quieter. She wondered what Eli was up to. After all, this wasn't like him. Eli wasn't the evasive type.

Melody rounded a corner and continued down the hall toward the palace library. The door was cracked open, and the orange glow of a fire danced within. Someone must have lit the fireplace. Her heart soared; she had always wanted to show Eli the palace library. Perhaps he beat her to it.

"Melody! I'm here!" Eli's voice called from within the library.

"I'm coming!" Melody called, running down the hall and bursting through the door.

As she supposed, the fireplace in the library was roaring heartily, casting its burning light all over the room. It was a spacious library, with books lining every wall. Several rows of bookshelves were in the back of the room where the fire's light was dim. Melody expected to see Eli somewhere inside, waiting for her with open arms and his brilliant smile.

But he wasn't there.

The white-bearded elder was sitting in an armchair facing the fire, with a large book on his lap, appearing to be reading. At Melody's sudden entrance, he looked up at her and they exchanged startled glances.

The elder said, "Oh, Milady! What a pleasure to see you. Is something the matter?"

"Uh, no, I, uh…" Melody took a few steps back. "I was just…"

"You look troubled," the elder said, gesturing to an armchair nearby. "Come, sit down."

Melody hesitated at first. But after looking around and seeing no one else in the room, and then glancing at the elder's concerned expression, she went and sat in the armchair.

"You cannot sleep, I presume?" the elder asked, marking his place in the book and closing it.

Melody nodded. "I was…I thought…well…" She couldn't bring herself to mention Eli.

"Milady, don't worry, I know what ails you. It's that renegade peasant, isn't it? The so-called Prince of Marindel?"

"He *is* the Prince of Marindel!" Melody snapped.

The elder coolly played along. "Oh, yes, of course. You know him better than I, so I'll take your word for it."

Melody's gaze settled on the warm fireplace. Questions cycled through her mind. *Why did Eli lead me here? Where is he? Is it all just my imagination? Maybe he's playing games with me. No, he isn't like that. I should just go back to bed.*

Melody was about to get up and leave when the elder cleared his throat and said, "You know, Milady, I'm sorry I've been so narrow-minded concerning him. If he is your preferred suitor, then by the royal laws of the kingdom of Rhema, your appointed officials ought to accept and support your decision."

Melody looked at the elder with wide-eyed shock. "What? Really?"

"Yes. After all, perhaps a married alliance between the kingdoms of Rhema and Marindel would be most strategic on our part during this troubling time in our history."

"Thank you," Melody nodded, grateful yet puzzled. "I can't believe it. Why did you change your mind?"

"Eli and I have little in common, as you know. I won't go into detail about that. But I've decided it isn't appropriate for your officials to keep you from making this decision for yourself. You are the queen, after all. It's our duty to serve and advise you, not to control you."

"I can still hardly believe it," Melody said, unable to keep from smiling. But then she remembered what Eli told her: that he soon had to leave for Marindel, and she couldn't come with him. The thought caused her smile to fade into a sullen frown.

"Hmm." The elder studied Melody's face. "You don't look as thrilled as I would have thought. You two have spent much time together. Has he not expressed his desire to marry you?"

"Yes, he has," Melody replied. She opened her mouth to speak again, but her lip quivered and nothing came out.

Melody saw it play through her mind over and over: the sorrowful Eli telling her he had to leave. Her heart grew heavier by the second. She remembered other things Eli said, but her heart's slippery hold on those memories was torn by the crafty Serpent, who spoke through her thoughts, *He doesn't love me. I am unlovable. I don't deserve someone like him, and that's why he's leaving me. He changed his mind about marrying me, so he's looking for a way to escape.*

Melody internalized every word.

Finally, she said to the elder, "Eli is going to leave. He says he wants to marry me, but he's going back to Marindel first—without me. He wouldn't tell me why."

The elder looked disappointed. "That is strange behavior, coming from a prince. He won't take you with him?"

Melody shook her head.

"I'm terribly sorry, Milady," the elder reached out to put a hand on her shoulder. "I can only imagine what it must have been like; led on by an amazing man for several weeks, just to have him suddenly run off to his next adventure as if nothing ever happened. Your heart must be in so much pain."

"It hurts, it hurts so much." Melody teared up as she continued. "Every night, I have nightmares of Eli letting me down. He hadn't let me down before, so I always thought they were just dreams. But after that night, when he said he'd leave me…what if…what if he never comes back? I don't think I can handle it! How can he do this to me? I've never loved *anyone* as much as I love him. Why is he taking me for granted?" By the time these words came out, Melody was sobbing.

"What a shame. I hate to see you in so much grief. Please, tell me, is there anything I can do to help?"

"I don't know!" Melody snapped. "Make him stay! Tell him he has to marry me right now, or not at all!"

"Ooh," the elder winced. "That's a very rash decision, Milady. I understand you're upset, but I'd advise you to think longer about a course of action like that. Think of the implications! What—"

"No," Melody interrupted. "I've thought plenty about it already. Eli says he loves me, but he can't just *say* things like that without proving it. If he says he loves me but still has it in him to go back to Marindel without me, how can I trust him?"

"That is a very good point," the elder said, nodding slowly. "I'm sorry to say this, Milady, but it looks like my fears about Eli are materializing all too quickly. From the very beginning, I've seen his reckless and unrefined nature, and it has made me very reluctant to trust him— not for my sake, but for yours. After all, it's our duty as your appointed officials to advise and protect you at all costs."

Melody sniffled.

"You must know that everything we do is for you," he continued. "We've been at odds with Eli because we saw his potential to hurt you, and we couldn't bear the thought of it. We love you, Melody, too much. We would hate to lose you to someone who would take you for granted."

"Do you really mean that?" Melody asked, looking up at him. She was particularly caught off guard when he called her 'Melody' instead of 'Milady.'

"Every word. You are our queen. Without you, what would we be? Our sole reason for existing is to serve you. It may not always be in ways you like or appreciate, but you must trust our judgment. We are *always* looking to protect your best interests, and the best interests of our kingdom."

Melody sat quietly, staring at the fire and pondering the elder's words as the last of her tears dried on her face.

The elder placed his hand on hers. When Melody looked at him, she was surprised to see his eyes had welled up. She had never seen him this emotional before.

"Melody," the elder said, "tell us where to find Eli. We will bring him in for questioning and determine his true intentions. If he wants to marry you, we will make it happen. And if not..."

Melody looked again at the fire. Her heart was torn. She wanted so badly to believe Eli at his word, but the storm in her soul was so chaotic, she couldn't bring herself to do it. She knew it was very unlike this elder to be so kind, and she remembered Eli telling her not to trust her officials. But now she didn't know whom to believe or whom to trust.

Questioning wasn't such a bad idea, after all. It seemed like a good place to start. If her officials could convince Eli to marry her and take her to Marindel with him, it would be more than she could ever ask for.

Melody took a deep breath before she spoke. "He spends the night in the countryside beyond the apple orchard, on a hill with a giant camphor tree."

"Very well," the elder nodded. "We will make preparations tomorrow, and in the evening, we'll set out to find him. In the meantime, please, go back to your room and get some rest. You've had a very emotional night."

"Thank you," Melody said, standing up. "Your help means so much to me. I'm sorry I've been so stubborn and rude."

"You are forgiven. Good night, Milady."

"Good night." Melody smiled and exited the room.

"Oh," the elder called as she left, "Please close the door behind you. I'm going to finish a chapter of my book before retiring to my quarters."

"Of course," Melody replied before shutting the door.

The elder opened his book to the marked page and began reading as before.

Several seconds passed.

Shadows moved in the back of the room as several figures emerged from behind the bookcases.

The elder spoke without lifting his gaze. "Did you hear that?"

"Every word," Matthias said, coming into the light of the fire. The figures behind him were his soldiers.

"We must handle this delicately. As enthusiastic as we are to dispose of Eli, we must do so with the perception of Melody's approval every step of the way. More importantly, we must avoid the public spotlight, or we risk the possibility of rebellion."

"Noted. What would you like us to do?"

"Send word to your soldiers at Point Nex. Have them prepare quickly and quietly. Tomorrow, at dusk, take your men and bring Eli here. We will do everything under cover of night while the city sleeps."

"Excellent," Matthias said with a cunning grin. He turned to his companions and said, "You heard the man. Rest up, eat your fill, and ready your weapons. When darkness falls tomorrow, we ride."

After returning to her room, Melody could hardly sleep. Nightmares tormented her every time she shut her eyes. She kept trying, even after the sun rose, but to no avail. At noon, she gave up and thought, *Maybe a nice walk around the city will help.*

She put on a simple tunic with a head shawl before leaving the palace. She took a roundabout way through smaller streets to the marketplace, which, to her surprise, was bustling more than usual.

This is odd, she thought. *Is there an important event today?*

As she made her way through the crowd, she heard shouting and jeering. Everyone was watching something just up ahead. She maneuvered through the crowd, eager to see what was going on. When she finally arrived at the front, she gasped in horror.

A giant Tethysian man was attacking Eli, who was on the ground and bloodied almost beyond recognition. The Tethysian sneered and laughed as he stomped on Eli's chest, saying, "You do not belong here! This realm is mine, and now you will pay the ultimate price!"

Melody recognized the voice, and it sent horrified chills down her spine. It was the voice of the Great Serpent.

As she stood there, unable to look away from the terrible sight, Eli turned his face toward her. Everything around her went quiet and even ceased to exist as Eli whispered, "Mel...*why*?"

Melody's vision went black, and she felt herself choking and gagging. She tried to scream, but the darkness was so thick, no sound came out of her mouth.

"No! No!" Melody flipped off the bed and landed with a thud, flailing about. When she realized where she was, Melody groaned and held her arm, which she had landed on, and stood up slowly.

She'd had many nightmares about Eli over the past few weeks, but this one was different. The image of Eli being tormented was seared in the forefront of her mind, and the slightest thought that it was her fault made her feel sick to her stomach.

When she remembered her conversation with the elder the night before, it struck her to the very core.

The Serpent said, using Melody's voice, *If Eli is hurt when your officials find him, it will be your fault.*

Melody bit her lip as she thought about it. She whispered to herself, "I didn't believe him. I don't believe him. I still don't. I hope...I..." She looked out her window, realized the time of day, and gasped.

Late afternoon. Sunset would take place in one hour.

Something in her heart told her she had little time to spare.

She thought aloud, "I don't care what the elder said. I know he doesn't like Eli, and there's no telling what kind of 'questioning' they're going to bring him into. I have to make sure they don't treat him unfairly."

With that, Melody put on an elegant white dress, which she reserved for important political meetings. She washed her face and fixed her hair, then went out to find her officials.

She searched the palace high and low. Every room, every hallway. Her officials were nowhere to be found. When she asked the palace guards, they said the officials left early in the morning and hadn't returned since.

After taking a moment to think, Melody decided it would be best for her to go to the camphor tree and tell Eli that her officials sought to question him. She asked the guards for a horse and set out immediately.

By the time Melody left Diamond City, the sun had set half an hour before. She skirted the apple orchard and rode northeast across the grassland, in the direction Eli had taken her on the unicorn. As the sky darkened with the coming of night, the landscape was different than it had been before. The grass was still, the fireflies were absent, and not a sound could be heard, except for the pounding hooves of Melody's horse. The moon had not yet risen, and most of the stars were veiled by wispy clouds above.

Melody thought little of her surroundings as she pressed onward. She hoped with all her might that she would reach Eli before her officials did. Maybe she could change his mind about leaving Rhema, and then they wouldn't have to question him. After all, the elder said they were willing to let her make her own decision.

When Melody reached the hill with the giant camphor tree, the horse whinnied defiantly and refused to go up, so Melody dismounted and ran the rest of the way.

Near the top, she saw Eli and two others on the far side of the tree trunk. At first, panic surged in her heart because she thought the two visitors were her officials. But then she slowed to a stop, eyes wide, because these visitors were radiant. She didn't recognize them, but there atop the mountain were two of the Galyyrim, speaking encouragement to Eli and strengthening him with their company. She could faintly hear their voices but couldn't discern what they were saying.

Melody rubbed her eyes in a daze, but when she looked again, the Galyyrim had vanished. She stood perplexed for a moment, not sure what to make of it. But at the sight of Eli alone on the hilltop, she cleared her thoughts and continued up to greet him. "Eli!"

He turned at the sound of her voice. It was too dark to see him well, but Melody could tell by his countenance that he was despondent. Nevertheless, he smiled and greeted her. "Melody, it's good to see you."

Melody ran straight into his arms and held him tight. She nuzzled her face in his hair and kissed his cheek. "It's good to see you, too."

After they separated, Eli said, "Mel, it's time for me to go."

"No, it's not," Melody blurted. She checked herself and clarified, "Eli, *please* don't go. I can't bear it. My officials have finally agreed to let us marry. Isn't that good news? Take me with you! Please, I beg you! What's stopping you now?"

Eli was silent for a while, and he choked up. Now that Melody was mere inches from his face, she could see the pain in his eyes. He reached up and stroked her face. "Melody, never forget. Please, never forget."

"Never forget what?" Melody pressed.

"How much I love you."

They stared into each other's eyes for a moment.

The night was silent, and the whole realm held its breath.

"I won't forget," Melody whispered. "I promise."

Eli's voice trembled as he spoke. "When you fully understand my love and call for my return, I will come for you."

Melody didn't know what he meant, but she nodded. "I *won't* forget."

Eli smiled once more, several tears streaming down his face, as he pulled away from Melody and took several steps back.

Melody's eyes widened. "Wait! You're not leaving *now*, are you?"

Eli said nothing.

The sound of rushing wind broke the silence of the night. A stream of fire came down from the heavens and carved a wall of flame between Melody and Eli.

Melody jumped back with a yelp and looked around wildly. She heard the wingbeats and snarls of dragons coming from every direction in chorus with the jeering shouts of men.

Another stream of fire drew a circle around Eli, trapping him in a flaming arena. Three talongrunts landed inside, each mounted by a Tethysian soldier. Two larger wyverns landed next. Each russet-brown frightwings carried four soldiers. The Tethysians dismounted and drew their weapons, and together they and their dragons surrounded Eli, taunting and snarling.

Another dragon arrived, and the ground shook with its landing.

161

This one, a thunder-beast, was burly and fearsome, resembling a winged black crocodile with a blunted snout and horns like a bull. Matthias rode proudly on its back. With a wave, he shouted, "Good evening, Prince Eli! Fancy running into you out here!"

Eli looked steadily at Matthias. "There's no need for a show. What do you want?"

Matthias slid down from his dragon's saddle and stepped forward. "We're looking for a wanted man who's guilty of sorcery, inciting rebellion against the Tethysian Empire, and falsely claiming to be the prince of a nonexistent kingdom. You know him?"

"What is this rebellion you speak of?" Eli asked.

Melody was overwhelmed with panic. She could but partially understand what was happening on the other side of the fire, which was too hot to approach, and she had a dreadful feeling about it all. She yelled, "Captain Matthias, stop! I command you as the Queen of Rhema to stop this now!"

Matthias responded to Eli, "The rebellion I speak of is shouting on the other side of the fire, telling me to stop. You've turned her against the will of the Empire, and for that alone, not to mention everything else you've done, you are worthy of the most excruciating death."

Melody didn't hear what Matthias said, but a surge of indignation came over her. She marched toward the ring and extended her hand forward, causing a magical blue divide to part the fire like a curtain as she passed through. She stood among the Tethysians and repeated, "Matthias, I command you as the Queen of Rhema to stop this immediately!"

The Tethysians were agape at Melody's use of magic and muttered amongst themselves, "She's a sorceress! That troublemaker has taught her how to use his powers! This can't be good! We must arrest her too!"

"Melody!" Eli called before anyone could address her. "Stand down. It's all right."

"What do you mean, it's…?" Melody trailed off as she looked at Eli's face, as loving and kind as ever, but with a stubborn determination that couldn't be moved. He said, "I must go with them; it's the will of the Great King. Go far away from here and be safe. The forces of darkness have come to eclipse the light, but soon the light will return. Be strong, Mel, and always, *always* remember my love for you."

"Eli…" Melody said as she stood wide-eyed and mouth agape. She couldn't bring herself to move, let alone speak.

Matthias grabbed the front of Eli's tunic and pulled his face up close. "You taught that woman sorcery!? How dare you defy the Empire by equipping its enemies with forbidden dark arts such as your own! Now, we will have to dispose of her, too!" He shoved Eli to the ground, eliciting a chorus of laughter from his troops. Then he looked at Melody and said, "I don't know what *you're* upset about, Princess. Your officials sent us to capture him after *you* so kindly told them where to find him. What's more, tonight, you led us right to him. We couldn't have caught him without you!"

Fear and extreme guilt flooded Melody's soul as she realized the danger she put Eli in. Her most recent nightmare was beginning to come true, and it really *was* all her fault!

Matthias continued, "Yet, after all you've done to help us catch your phony prince, still you stand before me in defiance of the mighty Tethysian Empire. I believe, when Emperor Flavian hears about this, he will allow us to make a smoldering ash heap out of the kingdom of Rhema. That would be fun, wouldn't it, boys?"

The soldiers snickered in agreement.

"Matthias," Eli said, standing up, "If you take me, you must leave Melody alone."

"You're in no position to bargain!"

Eli took one step toward Matthias, and by some invisible force, all of his men, and even the dragons, stumbled and fell. He said, "I'm the one you're looking for! Take me and do what you must, but you will leave Melody alone."

Matthias was taken aback. After composing himself, he said to his men, "What are you doing on the ground? Get up! Move the girl aside and bind the traitor!"

"No!" Melody pleaded. "Eli, don't!"

Eli looked at Melody with a loving smile. "Remember."

A Tethysian punched Eli in the face, forcing him to the ground. "No! No!" Melody ran toward Eli, but a talongrunt grabbed her with its talons and tossed her backward, sending her tumbling down the grassy hill.

After scrambling to her feet, she looked up to see flames on the ground extending their reach into the canopy of the camphor tree. Meanwhile, the dragons took to the sky, illuminated by the raging inferno, with their riders shouting and laughing in triumph. She saw Eli dangling from the talons of Matthias' thunderbeast as they disappeared into the murky darkness of the night.

"Eli!" Melody cried, falling to her knees and weeping uncontrollably.

Comprehension

1) List three ways in which the elder is able to gain Melody's trust. What valuable information does she give him?

2) Why must the elder and Matthias carry out their plan with the perception of Melody's approval?

3) How is Melody's latest nightmare different from those previous?

4) Why do the soldiers claim that Melody ought to be arrested? How does Eli respond? Why is that significant?

Reflection

1) How is Melody similar to Judas in this chapter? How is she similar to Peter? How are Judas and Peter similar in the betrayal of their loyalty to Jesus? How are they different?

10

Penumbra
Summer, 104 IE

Melody felt something nuzzle the back of her head. She groaned and rolled over, rubbing her groggy, tear-stained eyes. She blinked a few times before she recognized the snout of her horse, hovering inches above her face.

Upon seeing her stir, the horse snorted and nuzzled her again.

"Ugh, stop, stop it," Melody said, pushing the horse's snout away and sitting up. She rubbed her eyes once again before looking around. It was a gloomy, overcast day. The air was thick and humid, and there was a grim silence that could be felt.

"I must have cried myself to sleep," Melody said. When she saw the blackened remains of the camphor tree standing atop the scorched hill, she remembered what had happened. With a gasp, she jumped to her feet. "It's daylight already! Who knows what those horrible Tethysians might have done to Eli by now? I have to go back and help him right away!"

What's the use? The Serpent's words intruded on her thoughts. *You trusted your officials with Eli's location, and they gave him over to*

Matthias and his men. This is all your fault. You should have trusted Eli, but now it's too late.

Melody internalized the venomous accusation. "This is my fault. I never should have told my officials anything about Eli. I should have known they were up to no good." She took a deep breath and looked toward Diamond City, just on the horizon. "I have to help him. I can fix this. I'm the Queen of Rhema. I can fix this."

Something rustled in the grass nearby.

She looked and saw nothing; the grass was still. She heard it again from another direction, but again, there was nothing. A faint snickering noise seemed to jeer at her confusion.

"Stupid jackals," Melody muttered. Swallowing her fear, she swung herself onto the horse and urged it forward at a quick gallop. On the journey, Melody thought through what she could do to rescue Eli. She also kept an eye out for the jackals. For some reason, she couldn't shake the feeling that she was being watched.

Arriving in Diamond City, Melody sensed that something was off. The city was bustling as usual, but everyone seemed more fearful and skittish. When they saw Melody coming, they avoided eye contact and shuffled out of the way. She was disconcerted by their behavior but tried her best to ignore it and continued on horseback to the palace.

When she arrived at the gate, she asked the guards stationed there, "Where's Eli?"

The guards exchanged fearful glances but said nothing.

"What have they done to him?" Melody pressed. "Where is he?"

"Y-you're serious? You don't know?" one of the guards asked.

"I just got here. Please tell me."

The guard cleared his throat and explained, "Eli was arrested last night. The Tethysians and your officials came together here and put him on trial. He was unanimously sentenced to death."

Melody gasped. "What!? No! This isn't right at all! This isn't what I wanted!"

The guard backed away two steps. "Er, that's the interesting thing, Milady. The officials made it clear that *you* gave the order for his arrest. They made sure everyone in the city knew this was *exactly* what you wanted."

"What?" Melody realized the people were afraid of her when she arrived because they thought she betrayed Eli. She fumbled for words, "N-no, that's not what I wanted at all! I was just…I…I wanted Eli to stay! And the elder, he…! No! Oh, no!" Melody broke down in tears. "What have I done!?"

The guards exchanged glances again before slinking into the palace.

"Melody!" a familiar voice called from inside the gate.

She looked and saw Caruso coming toward her, bustling past the guards as they left. He looked distressed, but nevertheless, glad to see her.

"Caruso!" Melody slid off her horse and ran to embrace him. She wept and said, "It's all my fault, it's all my fault!"

Caruso held her tight and said, "There, there. Don't be hard on yourself. It's all a terrible misunderstanding."

"Did you see him? Were you here when it happened?"

"Yes. I was a part of the council the governor called upon for the trial last night. I tried to have him set free, but…" He shook his head and sighed.

"Where is he?" Melody asked. "Is he still alive?"

"Yes, but not for long. They flew off to Point Nex an hour ago. He'll be dead before the sun sets, I reckon."

Melody knew what Caruso meant by Point Nex. It was an isolated ocean bluff on the eastern coast of Rhema, which the Tethysians used for execution by means of a local sea monster, called Nex. The Tethysians trained Nex to come to the bluff at the sound of a certain gong. They would watch as the prisoner, bound near the cliff's edge, was tortured by the monster's secretion of flesh-dissolving acid and subsequently eaten. It was a punishment reserved for Rhema's most dangerous criminals. She asked, "What are we going to do?"

"I'm not sure there's anything we *can* do. Melody, I'm so glad you weren't here to see the way they treated him. Even well-esteemed Tethysian aristocrats I know personally acted like animals, yelling and chanting and spitting at him. And the soldiers! They were a terrible disgrace to the Empire, and even to the human race itself! They beat Eli without mercy until he could hardly stand. Then they forced him to face Matthias' thunder-beast in the courtyard, mocking him and telling him to sing to it. Eli stood his ground even as that bully of a dragon knocked him down, time and time again. If it weren't for the governor, Matthias and his men would have killed Eli then and there. Your officials stood by and cheered from the sidelines as if it were a bullfight. Everyone was stark-raving mad! It's as if a greater power has taken control of their minds to destroy that one man."

Melody wept as she listened to Caruso's words. When she finished, she whimpered, "It's all my fault. I have to do something. I won't be able to live with myself if Eli dies because of me."

"Don't say that. You know Eli wouldn't want you to think that way."

Melody nodded absently, hardly having heard him. She was thinking as hard as she could of a way to save Eli. An idea came to her as quick as a lightning bolt. "Caruso! Where's Hunter? Can I borrow him?"

"He's…well, actually, he escaped last night. With all the ruckus caused by Matthias' dragons, he and Kaya flew the coop. They could be anywhere by now."

Melody took Caruso by the arms and said, "I *need* him! Right now! Caruso, if I can make it to Point Nex before Eli is killed, I can sing to Nex and stop it from attacking him. You know I can do it—you saw me tame Kaya! Then I can turn Nex on Matthias and his cronies to get rid of them. It'll work if I get there in time, and Hunter might be the only dragon fast enough!"

"Nex has a much worse temper than Kaya, I'll tell you that," Caruso said, shaking his head in disbelief. "And there's no guarantee you'll get there in time, even with Hunter's help. Are you sure about this?"

"Yes. I have to try."

"All right then. I'll call Hunter, but he may be too far off to hear it."

"Please, just do it!"

"All right, all right! Here goes nothing." Caruso put two fingers

171

in his mouth and whistled.

After a few seconds, Melody asked, "How long will it take?"

"It depends on how far he is. Perhaps ten seconds, perhaps ten minutes."

"Oh, I hope he knows to hurry!"

"Well," Caruso glanced around, "I'm afraid I have to go back in to finish a report on the trial. I came out here for a short breather, you see. Go with Hunter and do what you must. I wish you luck, Melody." Caruso nodded goodbye and went inside the palace.

As he left, Melody searched the cloudy sky for any sign of Hunter. She tapped her foot and twirled a lock of her hair with impatient suspense.

It's no use, the Serpent mocked. *Try as you might, you will not be able to rescue Eli. All of Rhema will remember the role you played in his tragic and most untimely death. And they will utterly despise you.*

"No," Melody said to herself, still unaware it was the Serpent speaking in her mind. "I can fix this. I know it's my fault, but there's still time. I have a plan, and it's going to work."

The only reply was the eerie snickering Melody heard earlier in the countryside, accompanied by scuffling and rustling. She froze and looked around, listening intently. It seemed to be coming from several places nearby.

"Jackals wouldn't have followed me into the city," Melody muttered, anxiety welling up in her heart. What could be making that noise, if not jackals?

"Hello?" Melody called out. "Is anyone there?"

Two snickers answered her from opposite directions. The scuffling continued.

Melody stood as still as a deer as she observed her surroundings. No one was around, not even her horse; it had left while she spoke with Caruso.

A distorted voice whispered, "You betrayed him."

Out of the corner of her eye, she saw movement. She looked but saw nothing more than the shadow cast by the rampart near the palace gate.

"Who's there?" Melody squeaked.

"You are to blame," another distorted voice answered.

"No!" Melody yelled, running away from the palace gate and into the midst of the crowded buildings. Even then, she couldn't seem to escape the scuffling and snickering. It was coming from everywhere all around her. To make things worse, she thought she saw movement in every shadow she passed.

"Stop following me!" Melody yelled.

"You cannot escape your guilt!" a voice answered.

Up ahead, a shadow detached from a bulletin board and raced across the street into a dark alley. Melody skidded to a halt, and with trembling breath, she said, "If this isn't sorcery, I don't know what is. Show yourself!"

"You don't remember us?" several voices asked together. "We

remember you. We're altogether like you: servants of the Great Serpent."

Melody gulped. "I-I don't know you, and I'm nothing like you."

Derisive laughter was the only response.

Melody backed away from the alley where the shadow had gone. When she turned to go back to the palace, she saw movement in another shadow behind a crate. She watched with horror as a creature materialized out of the darkness.

It had the overall likeness of a baboon, standing four feet tall, with its body and long arms covered in mangy black fur. It had bulging white eyes, a pudgy snout like that of a pig, a crown of bony spines on its head, a set of locust-like wings on its back, curved yellow claws, and a naked rat-like tail. As it crawled into the light, the creature's wings buzzed to create the rustling sound.

Melody was petrified, her face drained of all color. She'd never been interested in folk legends, but if she had been, she would've recognized it. It was a creature from ancient ghost lore: the lukúba.

It spoke with a voice like grating stone, "What's the matter—scared?"

Melody screamed and turned away but quickly realized that three more lukúba had appeared behind her. She was surrounded!

"Leaving so soon?" they taunted, snickering and bearing their hideous, rotting fangs. "Stay with us, and enjoy the dying of the light."

"Leave me alone!" Melody shouted, voice trembling as she whirled around, looking for any means of escape.

The sound of a rushing wind echoed over the rooftops, followed by a fierce dragon yowl. Hunter dropped out of the sky like a preying eagle, and he collided with three of the lukúba. The impact sent them tumbling down the road with shrieks of surprise.

Hunter skidded to a stop, wings flared open wide, and motioned with his head for Melody to get on.

She wasted no time, breaking into a sprint toward Hunter. Hearing the snarls of the first lukúba as it gave chase, Melody leapt onto the dragon's back and clung to the saddle for dear life. "Go, go, go!"

Hunter yowled and turned, thwacking Melody's pursuer with his tail, before taking several bounds and launching upward. He flew straight into the cloud cover and disappeared from sight.

The lukúba got up from where they'd fallen, their bodies regenerating from broken bones and other injuries. They erupted with a chorus of laughter as they disappeared into the shadows from whence they came.

Around the same time Melody had woken up in the countryside, the Tethysian soldiers and Melody's officials arrived with Eli at Point Nex.

Just as Matthias had ordered, the seaside arena was prepared ahead of time for Eli's arrival. The granite-paved plaza was three hundred feet in diameter, with a two-hundred-foot drop, down jagged ocean cliffs, on one side. Tall, forested mountain crags flanked every other.

At the back of the plaza, several wooden bleachers and dragon landings had been set up. Spectators could watch the execution from a safe distance. The bleachers were adorned with Imperial Tethysian banners. Many Tethysians, and even a few Rhemans, already sat waiting.

At the front of the plaza, close to the cliff, there was an elevated granite platform. It was ten steps high. The only feature on top was a thick, wooden frame. Two poles stood about twenty feet tall and fifteen feet apart, with a third pole bridging across the top. There was a set of chains and shackles hanging down the middle. The frame was adorned with skulls and bones of every sort, from human to goblin to dragon.

Off to the side was an enormous gong, about twelve feet in diameter, with a black skull painted in the center.

Seagulls and vultures circled the site and rested in the high crags, waiting for the grisly show, soon to come.

A group of dragons, carrying prominent Tethysian and Rheman officials, crested the mountain crags and glided down toward the arena. They landed on the dragon platforms and let their riders down. Upon their arrival, the crowd began to cheer.

Matthias and his thunderbeast, which held Eli in its talons, descended toward the center of the arena. The dragon dropped Eli from several feet above ground before landing with a skid and a proud grunt.

A Tethysian soldier ran out to greet Matthias. "Sir! The arena is prepared and ready, just as you ordered."

Matthias slid down from his dragon and said, "Good work. It looks better than I've ever seen it."

The soldier looked at Eli and winced at the sight of him: bruised and bloodied, eyes swollen shut, clothes torn, and lying motionless on the ground.

Matthias followed the soldier's gaze and scoffed. "Don't worry about him. He's the Prince of Marindel; he can take a beating."

"Forgive me, sir, but will he bleed to death waiting for Nex to come? He looks like he's been mauled by a dragon."

Matthias chuckled. "Oh, you should've seen it!"

The thunderbeast snorted, eyes gleaming with amusement.

The soldier paused. "I suppose I should have. Shall we commence the execution, then?"

"Yes. Get your men over here and have the prisoner bound to the altar."

"Right away, sir." The soldier turned and ran back to the bleachers.

Matthias stepped onto one of his dragon's forelegs and held onto a spine while pointing at the bleachers. The thunderbeast jumped and flew to a vacant landing platform while Matthias rode on its arm.

Two of Melody's officials, the elder with the white beard and the other with the big nose, staggered toward Matthias, as though drunk.

"I don't know how you Tethysians do it," the white-bearded elder said between breaths. "I never want to fly on a dragon ever again."

"Quit your whining. Take a seat and enjoy yourselves; our hard work is about to pay off."

"I hope so," the big-nosed elder said. "I feel rotten."

"I don't want to hear it," Matthias said, barging past them and heading toward the top of the bleachers, where distinguished guests were allowed to sit.

The elders followed, complaining and bickering amongst themselves.

Meanwhile, three Tethysian soldiers ran out onto the plaza toward Eli. Two of them got on either side of him, picked him up, and dragged him toward the altar. The third soldier ran straight for the altar to ready the chains.

As they were dragging him, one of the soldiers asked in a whisper, "Eli, can you hear me?"

Eli opened his eyes and looked at him.

"I'm sorry about all this," the soldier said, voice trembling. "It's not fair. Prisoners of the Empire, even those condemned to die, are supposed to be treated with honor and dignity. Not like this. I...I do believe you're the Great Prince of Marindel. There's no other reason why they'd be doing this to you. Please, forgive us."

"You can't be serious," the second soldier scoffed, having overheard. "This bastard is getting exactly what he deserves." He addressed Eli. "You hear me, you piece of shit? You're getting *exactly* what you deserve! Every bit of it!" He jabbed Eli in the ribs with his elbow, eliciting a gasp of pain.

"Stop it!" the first soldier scolded. "Don't forsake your honor as an imperial soldier! We're better than that."

"Hmph. It's *because* we're better that we must crush our enemies without mercy!" The second soldier jabbed Eli in the ribs again.

Eli cleared his throat and coughed up blood. Then he said to the first soldier, "I hear you, and I will forgive you. The Great King welcomes you with open arms as his son." He turned to the other soldier and said, "And you will see with your own eyes the master of darkness, and then you will die."

Neither of the soldiers had time to comment because they arrived at the steps of the altar as Eli finished speaking. The third soldier helped them carry Eli up the steps and on a wooden stool to reach the chains. They shackled his wrists, then they removed the stool to let him hang. Once Eli was secure, they jogged back to the bleachers.

When the Tethysian officials saw Eli in place, they gave a nod to the executioner, who then stood on the highest platform of the bleachers where everyone could see him. He raised his hands in the air as a signal for everyone to be silent. Within seconds, a hush fell over the entire assembly.

The executioner began, "Privileged and highly-valued citizens of the Tethysian Empire, hear my words! You have, no doubt, gathered here today to witness the execution of a very prominent criminal: the traitorous Eli, the Great Prince of Marindel!"

Many in the crowd laughed at the executioner's evident sarcasm.

"This man is guilty of sorcery on many accounts. And for inciting rebellion within the kingdom of Rhema, not the least of which includes turning Queen Melody against the Imperial Tethysian crown." The crowd booed. Some shouted, "Long Live Emperor Flavian!" and "Long Live the Empire!"

"What you are about to see, valued citizens, is one of the many punishments for disloyalty and treachery within the domain of Emperor Flavian the Bright. May this carnal display serve as a dire warning: let not even your own thoughts cause you to betray the Tethysian Empire, or you will suffer this very same fate." He paused, and then shouted more passionately, "But, in addition, may you be endlessly entertained by the misery of this traitor at the jaws of the king of the southern sea, the mighty sea monster, Nex!"

The crowd cheered, some shouting, "Strike the gong!" and others chanting, "Long Live Emperor Flavian!" and, "Long Live the Empire!"

The executioner let the crowd go on for a moment before he gestured toward the gong, where a man stood wielding an enormous mallet. At the signal, the man hefted the mallet and struck the gong. The sound emanating from it was jarring. It echoed off the near-by crags and continued on for many seconds before it dissipated.

The crowd sat with bated breath, scanning the surface of the sea for any sign of Nex's arrival. Melody's officials, who had never seen an execution like this, were on the edge of their seats. The white-bearded elder, in particular, bit his nails with suspense.

The wind changed first.

It blew in from the sea, a stale and foreboding wind that rustled the trees in the mountains, creating an ominous whisper to accompany the pounding of the waves on the cliff.

The sky grew dark. The cloud cover thickened until it was as dark as twilight.

The vultures and the seagulls took to the sky and fled. Not even the gulls cried as they left.

The dragons grew restless. They crouched low on their platforms and whimpered, fidgeting and flicking their tails.

Matthias noticed even his prized thunderbeast was nervous. He narrowed his eyes. "Something's wrong."

The crowd began to murmur as an ocean swell appeared on the horizon. As it approached, those who had seen executions at Point Nex before stood and squinted their eyes. They muttered to themselves, "That's a very large swell." "Has Nex grown?" "What's happening?"

Eli hung from the chains on the altar, watching the swell as it loomed closer. Despite his condition, his eyes glimmered with determination. "Father, I trust you."

Suddenly, one of the talongrunts screeched in fright and took off. The noise triggered a similar reaction from all the other dragons, which roared and squealed as they fled, despite the surprised or reprimanding shouts of their owners.

The executioner glanced around with wide eyes as all these things took place. He looked at the incoming swell and declared with surety in his voice, "That's *not* Nex!"

Matthias watched as his dragon fled with the others, and then he looked at the swell in time to see the creature beneath come to the surface.

An enormous head rose out of the sea. The head of a fearsome, terrifying sea monster, with a crown of spikes all around its neck. It continued to rise, attached to a dark serpentine body, with seawater cascading down from every crevice of its mask-like face. The beast towered over Point Nex, its head alone half the size of the plaza. With bloodthirsty green eyes, it peered at the tiny spectators on the bleachers. Then, it bared its teeth in a grin and roared many times louder than the gong, which sounded moments before.

At the sight and sound of this monster, everyone was struck

with sheer terror. A third of them, including Matthias, fainted on the spot. The rest, including Melody's officials, scrambled and tumbled over each other, shouting and screaming for their lives as they fled behind the bleachers and between the mountain crags, down the only footpath out of Point Nex.

The soldier who mocked Eli, in his haste to escape, tripped down the bleacher steps and split his skull on the granite plaza. What Eli had said about him came to pass. This monster was none other than the master of darkness, the Great Serpent himself.

Comprehension

1) Why are the people of Diamond City afraid of Melody?

2) What does Caruso conclude about Eli's trial? Why is this significant?

3) What is Melody's plan to save Eli?

4) Describe how prisoners are executed at Point Nex.

5) Why does Eli say that one of the soldiers carrying him will be forgiven, and the other will die?

Reflection

1) How much pain (physical suffering) and shame (psychological and social suffering) would you endure to rescue someone or something you love or to support a cause you believe in? Why would you do this?

2) Read Isaiah 53:4-7, Mark 15:16-20, and Luke 22:63-65. As you reflect on these accounts of Jesus willingly enduring pain and shame on your behalf, what emotions are brought up? Do you feel worthy of his suffering? Why or why not?

11

Umbra
Summer, 104 IE

Hunter and Melody soared through the clouds, having just escaped from the lukúba. After catching her breath, Melody said, "You were just in time. Thanks for saving me."

Hunter chirped pleasantly.

"We need to get to Point Nex right away. Do you know how to get there?"

Hunter grunted, steering left, so they were headed in that direction.

"Good. I can't see anything in these clouds, so I won't be able to guide you. But you need to fly fast, all right? As fast as you can!"

They flew on for a few moments with no interruptions. Melody was too focused on her mission to notice when the atmosphere changed, but Hunter wasn't. He slowed to a glide and sniffed the air to check their surroundings. When he picked up strange scents on the wind, he snarled.

Melody blinked. "Huh? What's wrong?"

A lukúba darted out of the clouds with a shriek, locust-wings buzzing, and tackled Hunter from the side. Hunter buckled in flight.

"Ah! Hey!" Melody shouted, holding the handles tight. She looked around for the creature, but after hitting the dragon, it had disappeared into the clouds. To their dismay, Melody and Hunter could hear buzzing and creepy laughter all around them.

"How were those things able to catch up? I don't like this, Hunter. See if you can—ah!"

Another lukúba latched onto Hunter's wing, and he struggled in flight. As the creature scratched and gnawed at his wing membrane, Hunter yowled and tried to throw it off.

Melody yelled, "Get off! Let go of my dragon!"

Hunter managed to free himself from the first lukúba, but only seconds later, two more came from opposite directions. One tried to go for Hunter's other wing, but he saw it coming and dodged. Meanwhile, the second one grabbed onto Hunter's flank and began crawling up toward the saddle.

Melody screamed, jumping and kicking her legs out behind her to hit the lukúba. The stunt was a direct hit, sending it flying back into the clouds from whence it came.

Another lukúba came from up ahead, braced for a head-on collision, but Hunter spun out of the way just in time. Melody crouched low on the saddle and hung on tight. After that, she said, "Hunter, we need to get out of these clouds. I think they can see us, but we can't see them. Can you fly up above?"

Despite the pain of his injuries, Hunter veered upward and began pounding the air with his wings. As they went, the jeering and buzzing of the lukúba echoed all around. It got louder and louder until it was almost deafening. Then, Hunter and Melody broke into a large cavern within the clouds.

To their horror, they beheld a massive swarm of lukúba. Hundreds of them, swirling like a vortex! Before Melody and Hunter realized what they'd just flown into, a handful of the creatures broke away from the swarm and careened toward them.

"Ah! Hunter! Fly! Fly!"

The dragon tucked, diving to achieve maximum velocity and escape the pursuing creatures. Plunging back into the clouds, he continued his rapid descent for a few seconds before pulling up to fly level.

It was no use.

Three lukúba tackled Hunter from the right side, and he rolled in flight. This time, Melody was thrown off the saddle and went hurtling into the abyss, screaming as she fell.

Hunter quickly reoriented himself and dove after her.

As Melody fell, a lukúba intercepted her and attempted to fly away with her. Melody didn't make it easy. She screamed and flailed about, kicking and punching at the creature. It squealed and hissed as it tried to subdue her, but soon it lost its grip. Less than a second later, Hunter snatched the lukúba and ripped it in half with his jaws.

Finally closing the distance, Hunter swooped underneath Melody so she could land on his back. She grabbed the saddle and clung to it, breathing hard and trembling. The terrifying fall left her feeling nauseous, and she yearned for the attack to be over.

But there was much more terror to come.

A lukúba grabbed the end of Hunter's tail, and two more clung to his underside. Creatures came in from everywhere, overwhelming Hunter until he was unable to fly. He tumbled downward, yowling and thrashing to free himself.

In the midst of it all, Melody did her best to throw off lukúba without letting go of the handles. She kicked several off before one perched in front of her and began pounding her with its fists, hissing and spitting in her face. She gagged on its putrid carrion-breath.

The two of them were so preoccupied, they hardly noticed when a fireball sliced through the clouds and struck the creatures on Hunter's tail. The resulting blast sent all but three of the lukúba hurtling off and out of sight.

Kaya swooped down with an indignant screech, picking off one of the remaining lukúba with her powerful talons. She tossed it toward an incoming lukúba, causing them to collide and spiral out of sight. Regaining his aerial balance, Hunter flicked the second-to-last lukúba off his wing. As Hunter's flight stabilized, Melody gained the courage to punch the face of the creature assaulting her. It lost its balance and fell into the clouds.

Hunter and Kaya exchanged happy chirps and grunts. Melody looked up and said, "Kaya, I've never been so happy to see you in my whole life."

Their celebration was short-lived. The two dragons flew head-long into an oncoming swarm of lukúba, and a battle ensued. The creatures maintained their strategy of clinging to the dragons to disable their flight. However, now that Kaya was present, neither dragon was overwhelmed for long. Kaya shot down lukúba with her dragonfire before they could attack Hunter. Likewise, Hunter veered, dove, and snatched any lukúba going after Kaya.

As much as Melody was impressed by the dragons' teamwork in aerial combat, she hadn't lost sight of her goal. During a lull in the attack, she said, "Hunter, Kaya, we need to hurry on to Point Nex. These things are distracting us while Eli is in trouble!"

The dragons chirped back and forth as if discussing a plan. Then Hunter turned and flew level in the direction of Point Nex. Kaya took a position above and behind Hunter so she could see any lukúba that might try to sneak up on him.

For a moment, all was quiet. Melody began to think they had finally escaped from the hideous creatures.

They came in from above, behind, and both sides. They were organized and precise. They'd been preparing their formation for some time out of sight, and now they performed flawlessly.

Four lukúba attacked Hunter, targeting his wings.

Kaya saw them coming and shot them down with a couple of fireballs.

While she was busy, five lukúba landed on her back and began tearing into the joints of her wings. She screeched and began flailing about to throw them off.

Before Hunter could turn to rescue her, six lukúba came from all directions and attacked him just as ruthlessly.

"No!" Melody screamed. For the first time ever, she was fearful for the lives of these dragons. Memories flashed in the forefront of her mind. She remembered her first impression of Hunter when she trespassed into Caruso's backyard. She remembered when Eli tamed him, and she tamed him as well. Melody remembered what a big deal it was for her to tame Kaya. It was an accomplishment she was very proud of. Then she recalled flying all over Rhema with Eli. Though she began that day hating all dragons, by the end of it, she'd grown especially fond of Hunter and Kaya. Eli helped her see their personalities, their loyalty, and their persevering nature.

Melody's eyes welled up as she realized the danger she had put Hunter and Kaya in. After all, they were only being attacked by the lukúba because of her. With a shout, she began fighting the lukúba nearest her with all her might.

It was no use.

Melody heard Kaya's blood-curdling shriek in time to see her fall into the clouds, hardly visible in a mob of lukúba.

"No! Kaya!"

Hunter let out a desperate cry as he also began to fall.

"Hold on, Hunter! Hold on! We have to go save Kaya! Come on, you can do it!"

A final shot from Kaya careened through the clouds and struck the creatures on Hunter's underside, causing most of them to tumble off. Hunter yowled with effort and performed a tight dive and corkscrew to fling off the rest of the lukúba, and then he stabilized and began to glide as best as he could.

Melody was shocked to see how badly Hunter was injured. His wing membranes were shredded and dripping blood, and his tail and neck were pock-marked with bites and gouges. His flight was shaky and unstable. He wheezed for every breath.

"Hunter, oh, Hunter!" Melody placed her hand on his neck. She paused, reflecting again on her role in the dragon's suffering, and she began to cry. "I-I'm sorry, I'm really sorry. I did this to you, and to Kaya. It's my fault. I was so stubborn, and so needy, and so…I'm sorry, Hunter! I'm—oh! Look out!"

As Melody spoke, the lukúba had descended out of the cloud cover, and now they were quickly approaching forested mountain crags. Hunter yelped, trying to maneuver out of the way, but he ripped through a tree on the mountainside and spun out of control. He was too injured, and falling too quickly, to reorient himself. A crash-landing was imminent. Melody shut her eyes and held on tight, knowing and accepting she'd probably not survive the impact.

Hardly a moment after the Serpent's grand entrance, Point Nex had been completely vacated. Only the unconscious remained, strewn about the bleachers and surrounding area as though dead.

The Serpent rumbled with contentment as he looked down on Eli, who was still chained to the altar. For the first time, the Serpent spoke aloud: "I've been waiting a long time for this day, mighty Prince. What a pleasure it is to see you in chains before me at last."

Eli revealed no hint of fear or surprise.

The Serpent continued, "Now, on this dreadful day, I will destroy Marindel once and for all by eliminating the only heir to the throne. Then I will become the Eternal Overlord of all things above and below the sea. How does that make you feel, Prince? I couldn't have done it without your naive cooperation and misplaced faith in that foolish human girl."

Eli winced with effort as he spoke. "You've become very powerful, Serpent, but pride will be your downfall. The Great King is not blind to your schemes, nor am I."

"Well then, you must already know what I have in store for you.

"Do you really believe that by killing me, you will have the victory?"

The Serpent chuckled. "Oh, you *are* clueless. My victory is certain. That is a given. Future generations will look back on this hour of history and tell with appropriate fear the story of the darkest of days. However, they will not speak of the Great Serpent killing the Great Prince. No. *I* will not be the one to kill you."

Eli stared at the Serpent, waiting for him to continue.

The beast glanced across the plaza and grinned, eyes twinkling maliciously. "*She* will."

Hunter's distant yowls echoed on the mountain crags, accompanied by the twisting of branches and the breaking of boughs. The dragon made his entry into Point Nex by crashing through the canopy of a large tree and scuffing the top of the bleachers. Dismantling the highest levels, he sent several Imperial banners to the ground. Upon Hunter's contact with the setup, Melody was thrown off the saddle and sent tumbling down the bleachers like a rag-doll. Hunter skidded and rolled on the granite plaza in a flurry of wings and limbs, and then was still.

Melody groaned, hugging herself pitifully. Her white dress was dirty and torn, and her hair was a windblown mess. She had bruises from the beating she endured from the lukúba and a few scrapes from her encounter with the bleachers.

Eli glared up at the Serpent. "I told you not to harm her!"

"She puts herself in harm's way," the Serpent purred. "That spoiled, selfish girl will do anything to get what she wants, and you know it."

Melody was roused by the Serpent's thundering voice. She'd gotten a mild concussion from the landing, and her senses were distorted. Groaning with effort, she sat up and observed her surroundings. There were the wrecked bleachers, at the foot of which she landed. She saw the bodies of those who had fainted strewn all around her. Beyond that, she saw Hunter's crippled body and gasped. "Hunter!" She tried to stand, but she was too dizzy and fell to her knees.

Looking beyond Hunter, across the plaza, Melody saw the altar. At the sight of it, she realized where she was and why she wanted so badly to arrive there. "Eli!" She moved to stand again but stopped immediately when she noticed a massive, dark shape beyond him. She slowly looked above and behind the altar, and through her blurred vision, she could just make out the terrifying face of the Serpent, leering down at her.

"Oh…my…" Melody's blood ran cold as the horrible memories of her first encounter with the Serpent flooded her mind.

The Serpent grinned. "Hello there, my beautiful friend. It's been a long time. I was beginning to miss you."

Though immensely frightened, Melody said, "It's…it's you! *You're* behind all this!"

"I'm flattered, but I must disagree. I'm only a spectator here. Eli and his daddy are behind all of this."

"No," Melody said, wobbling as she stood. "*You* started everything. *You* tricked me into releasing you. *You* turned everyone against Eli so he would be arrested. *You* sent those creatures after me and got

193

Hunter and Kaya killed. You've ruined my life, and now you're ruining his!" She noticed a spear next to a fainted soldier, and she went to take it. Then she looked at the Serpent and said, "You have to leave. As the Queen of Rhema, I order you to leave now and let Eli be."

The Serpent laughed, eyes glittering. He said to Eli, "Did you hear that? Your little girlfriend believes she can challenge me. There's only one problem with that, as I'm sure you're aware. She has no authority from Marindel to do so. She gave it to someone…me, I believe. Oh! And *you* gave up your authority as well, in a sad attempt to rescue her. Neither of you has any authority at all, yet here I am with all the power in the realm!"

"Leave her out of this. Your quarrel is with me."

While the Serpent was speaking, Melody heard the rustling and snickering of the lukúba. She looked around, and to her dismay, she saw them coming out of every shadow on Point Nex. Even high up in the crags, they perched in the treetops and hung on the cliffs. There were hundreds, if not thousands, of them. And they were closing in on her. Trembling with fear, Melody backed away from the lukúba, toward the altar. She held the spear in front of her as if it would help deter the fearsome horde.

The Serpent watched Melody with a low purr. He said to Eli, "Before you go, you must realize how misplaced your faith in your father is. He found it wise to dismiss *me* from the royal court. And then he turned and gave his inheritance to an abandoned human girl, unwanted even by her own parents. Do you not realize the fallacy of his wisdom? Do you not realize how easy it was for me to take that power away from her? Do you *really* believe that, by taking her punishment, you will make life better for her, or for any other creature in the realm? What an ignorant fool you are! As long as I have this power, I have the freedom—no, the right—to resist and destroy the Kingdom of Marindel, and your father freely gave it to me through that girl. Now, he is disposing of you, leaving the throne vacant for me to take. And believe me, I will gladly oblige. What further evidence do you need? Your father, the King, is not so great after all, is he?"

Eli replied, "You are wicked beyond redemption. You have no place among the Galyyrim in the presence of the Great King. Your powers are nothing more than death, darkness, and despair. Today, you reign in glory. But what have I told you? Even shadows must flee when the light comes. The power you stole will be taken from you once and for all, and returned not only to Melody, but to all who choose to follow the Great King. They will be sons and daughters in the royal court, but you and your kind will be destroyed forever."

"Hmhm, the words of a lunatic. If you will not believe me when I tell you of the power I possess, then I'll just have to *show* you." He maneuvered his face toward Melody, who stood a dozen feet away from the altar.

Melody froze in place. The sliver of boldness she had to challenge the Serpent earlier was vaporized by the enormous monster's scoffing gaze.

The Serpent's focus remained on Melody as he addressed Eli, "Witness now, glorious Prince, as the most devastating forces both above and below the sea come together in the soul of this weak and selfish creature you love so wrongfully. Witness now as my superior powers of darkness and chaos destroy every lie you've planted in her pathetic little brain and reduce her to the ruthless animal she truly is. Witness now, with fear and reverence, as the beloved daughter of the King bows before my sovereign might. Death will consume you as it consumes every mortal, and in the wake of your meaningless life, death will consume the entire realm under my command!"

The Serpent lowered his head so that his snout was at the edge of the seaside cliff. He summed up his monologue with one last phrase,

"Try as you might, dear Prince, there is no way to save her. The girl belongs to me."

At his words, the lukúba erupted with a raucous cacophony. They screeched and yowled, pounding their chests or the ground with their fists and picking up nearby items to bang together.

Spines on either side of the Serpent's head vibrated to emit a continuous high-pitched ringing. His brow furrowed and his pupils contracted as he focused on Melody, tilting his head slowly back and forth.

This chaotic racket was a twisted version of the Music of Marindel, conducted to achieve the opposite purpose. It was the Din of the Serpent.

Melody yelped and cringed, holding her hands to her ears and falling to her knees. The spear clanged to the ground beside her. The Serpent established a mental connection with her and drilled into her psyche, subduing all her positive thoughts and emotions to replace them with his own.

Melody screamed and thrashed about in vain resistance. Her will to trust Eli and remember his love hadn't been strong enough before. Now, under the destructive hypnotism of the Serpent, there was no hope. Melody was confronted with all her memories of Eli, including those from her nightmares, and they blended together as one.

Over the memory of Melody and the forbidden door, the Serpent reminded her, *Eli was not there to warn you. Your naivety is all his fault.*

Over the memory of Melody being tortured and cast out of Marindel by the Serpent asserted, *Eli was not there to protect you. Your pain and your exile are all his fault.*

Over the memories of Melody's first millennium on the surface, before she came to Rhema, the Serpent continued on, *Eli was not there to comfort you. Your loneliness and your misery are all his fault.*

Over the memories of the Tethysian occupation of Rhema, the Serpent accused, *Eli was not there to give wise counsel in your negotiations with the Empire. Your loss of freedom is all his fault.*

Over the memory of Melody's interaction with the pineapple farmer, the Serpent's words dug deep. *Eli humiliated you in front of your own people. You were left exposed to public ridicule. It's all his fault.*

Over the memory of Melody and Eli running from Matthias and his men in the village, the Serpent proclaimed, *Eli roused the fury of the Tethysian Empire against you. They will destroy you, and it will be his fault.*

Over the memories of Melody and Eli at the camphor tree, the Serpent tore into every word Eli said about leaving. *He doesn't care about you. He doesn't love you. He led you on this whole time. You were right to turn him in to your officials.*

Over many other memories, the Serpent imposed his lies and removed the small seedling of loyalty Melody had for Eli. At the same time, fed by the Din of the Serpent, Melody's fear, pain, and rage were amplified to new heights. Soon, she stopped resisting and lay still on the ground.

In the background, unbeknownst to anyone, Matthias was roused to consciousness by the noise. He looked up from his place on the ground and watched with terrified bewilderment as everything took place.

Once Melody's soul was subdued, the Serpent introduced the final thought: *Eli deserves to die. Kill him.*

"Eli deserves to die," Melody whispered, raising her head to look at him with unbridled hatred. Trembling under the weight of her emotions, she took up the spear, rose to her feet, and closed the distance between herself and the altar.

The lukúba screeched, howled, and pounded with a passionate frenzy. The Serpent looked on, his hypnotic gaze level with the plaza, eager not to miss a single detail. The climax was imminent.

Melody walked around the altar and into Eli's field of vision. Then she ascended the steps toward him.

When Eli looked into Melody's eyes and saw what the Serpent had done, tears began flowing down his face. Nothing hurt him more than seeing how much pain Melody was in.

When she reached the top of the steps, Melody took a deep breath and hefted the spear. Her words epitomized everything she sincerely believed at that moment.

"Eli, I hate you."

"Mel…" Eli sobbed. His anguished expression showed her words were a direct hit. But, in spite of his pain, he whispered, "I forgive you."

Melody plunged the spear into Eli's chest, through his heart, and out his back.

Eli gasped. His eyes stayed locked with Melody's for one more moment before he lowered his head.

The Din of the Serpent ceased. The forces of darkness held their breath.

Time stood still. The wind and the waves were silent. Not a

sound could be heard except for Melody's heavy breathing as she stood with a white-knuckled grip on the spear in Eli's body. Blood ran down the shaft of the weapon and onto her hands, even dripping down onto her soiled dress.

"He's dead." The Serpent maneuvered his massive head closer to Eli's body, with the tip of his snout only inches away, and sniffed to confirm his observation. He straightened his neck, towering over Point Nex once again, and declared with confidence, "The Great Prince is dead!" The lukúba laughed, cheered, and rustled their wings in chorus.

Upon hearing the Serpent's proclamation, the trance on Melody broke. She shook her head and blinked, taking a few seconds to realize where she was and what she was holding. She jumped away from the spear and stared agape at Eli, who she saw up close for the first time since his arrest on the hilltop. "Eli…! No…!"

The Serpent looked at Melody with a smug grin. "Yes, my darling, your eyes do not deceive you. The Great Prince is dead, and I have no one to thank more than you."

Melody's voice quivered, "H-how…how *could* you?"

The Serpent laughed. "'How could *I*?' How pathetic! Do you need me to spell it out for you? *You* killed him! *You* are to blame! He was condemned to die because of *you*!" He tore into Melody's psyche once again, causing her to feel the full weight of guilt and the ultimate responsibility for Eli's death.

Unable to bear the Serpent's tormenting accusations, Melody wept and wailed, clinging to Eli's dangling body and shouting, "No! Why!? I should have died instead! I deserve to die, not him! It's all my fault! It's all *my* fault!"

The Serpent was ecstatic. He said to his minions gathered all over Point Nex, "The Great Prince is dead! The sovereign reign of the Great Serpent, and the sovereign reign of death over every living thing, begins *now!*" The Serpent flexed his body and waved his tail fluke in the air as he roared long and loud in triumph.

The lukúba took to the air, screeching and howling with glee, and swarmed in a vortex around the Serpent as he roared.

Matthias, still on the ground and afraid to move, saw everything. There was only one thing he could say as he observed the terrifying celebration of the dark forces. "What have we done?"

Melody was still clinging to Eli and weeping when two burly lukúba came from behind to pry her away from the body.

"No! No!" Melody struggled to break free, but they were too strong. They dragged her down the steps and tossed her on the ground, laughing and spitting on her. Utterly defeated, Melody hid her face in her arms and sobbed.

The Serpent looked at Eli's body with a prideful sneer. "I mustn't allow my noble adversary to become carrion for the vultures. I will rid the realm of the sight of him." He opened his jaws and vomited a glob of sticky black tar onto the altar. The substance solidified within seconds. Then, the Serpent turned to Melody and lowered his head toward her, saying, "Oh, look at you, groveling on the ground like the useless worm you are! There is nothing great about you at all. Nothing special. There's no room in my dominion for a creature as hated and worthless as you. Give up all hope of ever ruling this kingdom, let alone living peacefully anywhere else. In my mercy, I will not kill you, but you will spend the rest of your long and useless life with me. After all, no one else will understand what you've done. I alone will keep you safe and out of trouble. In my very being, you will find rest."

He extended his forked tongue toward Melody. When it

touched her, hundreds of fleshy tendrils shot out and wrapped around her, cocooning and absorbing her into the Serpent's tongue. As this occurred, Melody was still. She only muttered to herself, "I *am* worthless. I deserve to die."

Once Melody was completely engulfed by the Serpent's tongue, he retracted it and straightened up again. To his minions he said, "My loyal followers, Rhema is ours! Let us enjoy ourselves and feast upon it!"

The lukúba howled and cheered. The swarm dispersed as groups of the creatures scattered everywhere, disappearing in the shadows. Their cackles were fading away as the Serpent said, "First, we will afflict Rhema. And then, all of Tyrizah."

At that, the Serpent looked up and ascended into the sky. His long, coiling body trailed behind him, showering Point Nex with a downpour of seawater as he passed over. His sinister laugh echoed off the crags as his dark form disappeared in the clouds above.

Comprehension

1) When the Serpent says, "You must realize how misplaced your faith in your father is," what example does he give? What does this imply about the Serpent's origin?

2) How is the Din of the Serpent different from the Music of Marindel?

3) Why is Melody unable to resist the Serpent's attack?

4) What are Melody's final words to Eli? How does he respond?

5) What happens to Melody at the end of the chapter?

Reflection

1) What do you notice about the Serpent's lies spoken to Melody before Eli's death, and those spoken after? How might Satan use this strategy to keep people trapped in cycles of sin and guilt?

Void
Summer, 104 IE

Matthias stayed on the ground for several hours after the dark forces departed from Point Nex. Finally, as his surroundings turned ebony with the coming of night, he mustered the strength to stand. He lit a torch and crossed the plaza to inspect the mound of tar concealing Eli's body.

He walked a complete circle around it. He noticed not a single portion of the altar was left uncovered, not even the steps.

He tapped it with his foot. It was definitely solid.

After looking about to make sure no one was around to see his curiosity and make fun of him, he placed the torch on the ground and drew his sword. Taking a deep breath and gripping it with both hands, he swung his weapon at the mound. The sword bounced off the tar with tremendous recoil, and with a shout of surprise, Matthias spun and fell to the ground.

Groaning with annoyance, Matthias stood and prepared to lunge at the mound again, but a spark of ingenuity caused him to pause. He sheathed his sword and picked up the torch. He held it up to the mound with the flame burning against the smooth, black surface to see if it would melt or catch fire.

"You there!" a voice called from across the plaza.

Matthias jumped, dropping the torch and turning around. A Tethysian cavalry had arrived, illuminated only by the lanterns they carried. As they approached, Matthias recognized them to be high-ranking military personnel from nearby Carnelian Cove. He supposed they'd been sent to scout the area after those who fled from the Serpent arrived and caused a scene. After all, anyone who'd never seen the Serpent wouldn't know to believe anyone who claimed there was a Serpent in the first place.

But Matthias knew.

He saw the way Eli died.

The lead officer asked, "What in the name of Flavian the Bright happened here?"

Matthias opened his mouth to speak, but no sound came out. He looked around, pointed at the mound, bumbled a few nonsensical words, and then his eyes rolled back, and he fainted.

The lead officer scowled. "Well, we shouldn't have expected an intelligent answer from *him*." To his companions, he said, "Round up the unconscious and wounded. Keep your guard up and your eyes open for those monsters."

That night was the longest and darkest night in the history of the kingdom of Rhema. By the power of the Great Serpent, a supernatural void sat heavily upon the island kingdom. The moon and stars failed to shine, and dawn never arrived.

The lukúba roamed freely, causing mischief and havoc in every village and city across the kingdom. Tremendous fear was in the hearts of all who saw and heard them. People shut themselves in their homes and barricaded the windows and doors to find refuge from the onslaught of terror. Undeterred, some lukúba flitted as shadows under the doors to torment those inside. They derived enjoyment from eliciting fear, vandalizing belongings, and provoking fights with anyone who sought to challenge them.

The Tethysians resisted the lukúba at first. But once they realized the monsters couldn't be killed, they too shut themselves in their fortresses and manors. Even the dragons hid. They sensed and feared the presence of the Great Serpent.

The Rheman officials, after finding their way back to Diamond City through the lukúba-infested grasslands, wanted nothing more than to hide in the palace and forget about the events of the past few days. However, only moments after they arrived—thirty-six hours after Eli's death—they were called by the palace guards to see something outside. Weighed down by a lack of sleep and haunted by the guilt of what they had done, the officials crept into the courtyard and onto the balconies. They stared up at the sky in horror.

The Great Serpent floated above Diamond City, all but blending in with the night, except for his fierce green eyes. Everyone in the city beheld the enormous beast, and they were paralyzed with fear. Once he had their attention, the Serpent said, "Citizens of Rhema, I have come to claim this kingdom that is rightfully mine. Eli is dead, and Melody is gone. There is no one left to protect you now. You *all* belong to me."

The Serpent opened his jaws to unleash a torrent of black sludge on the palace.

Comprehension

1) Why do you think Matthias is interested in the mound concealing Eli's body?

2) When the Serpent appears over Diamond City, for how long has Eli been dead?

Reflection

1) Describe a time in your life that felt like an endless night. Did you sense God's presence with you in those moments? If not, imagine yourself amid that hardship, with Jesus sitting right beside you. What would you say to Him? How does His presence there change your outlook on the situation?

Antumbra
Summer, 104 IE

Around that time, Caruso was prompted by the Great King to go to Point Nex and pay respects at the altar. He had barricaded himself in his manor to escape the lukúba, and the last thing he wanted to do was go outside. Caruso didn't know it was the Great King speaking to him then, and he had neither dragon nor horse to make the journey in good time. Nonetheless, he mustered what little courage he had and departed from the manor.

Even with the help of a lantern, he couldn't see more than five feet in front of him. Every fiber of his being willed him to turn back and hide. But ultimately his loyalty to Eli superseded every fear in his heart, even if only by a hair.

Just after he left the village, a unicorn galloped into view. It pawed the ground with a whinny, urging him to get on. Intrigued, Caruso mounted the unicorn and allowed it to take him to Point Nex. Lukúba tried to distract and intimidate them on the journey. But to Caruso's surprise, the creatures were unable to approach them. Confused and annoyed, the lukúba turned and squabbled with each other. Caruso's fear of the lukúba diminished over time, and he began to wonder what greater power was at work.

Arriving at Point Nex, the unicorn took Caruso to the mound where Eli's body was concealed. Caruso dismounted and looked sadly at the mound. He thought about Eli's life: everything he had said and done, the smile he always carried, his compassion for all people, and his determination in the face of hardship. The thoughts moved him to tears. "Eli, we desperately need you. We're facing a judgment we certainly deserve but can never hope to survive."

At the sound of approaching hooves, he turned and saw two more horses enter the plaza. He recognized them to be Eli's friends from Jasper Village: Auben, his wife Trisha, and their kids Trevor and Lia. Auben and the kids were on one horse, while pregnant Trisha was on the second.

Caruso greeted them with a nod as they came near. "It's a dark time to be out and about with kids."

"It'd be worse to leave them in a village crawling with monsters," Auben said as he dismounted. He turned to help his kids down and then went to help his wife.

Trevor ran toward his mother and hugged her leg. "Mom, where's Mister Eli?"

"Hush," Trisha caressed his head. She said to Caruso, "Auben and I had a strange feeling we were supposed to visit Point Nex. It was so unshakable we decided it must be significant. We took the kids and came as fast as we could."

"The same happened to me," Caruso said, stroking his chin. "How peculiar."

Seconds later, another man on horseback arrived; the pineapple farmer from Diamond City. Then, a talongrunt landed nearby, carrying the soldier who had apologized to Eli en route to the altar. Both men dismounted and joined the others, admitting the same premonition had come upon them as well.

Over the next few minutes, several others from all over the kingdom came and stood before the mound. The two things they all had in common were a belief in Eli as the Great Prince of Marindel, and a mysterious feeling that they needed to go to Point Nex, despite the rampant forces of darkness that plagued the land. Once they'd all gathered, they began wondering what they were supposed to do there.

"Maybe we can break this rock open and get Eli's body out," the pineapple farmer said. "Give him a proper burial."

"How do you suppose we do that?" Auben asked.

"I brought a hammer," a blacksmith said.

"My sword might do the trick," the soldier suggested.

"Hmm." An elderly lady knocked on the mound with her ear up close to it. "This substance is both solid and elastic. It won't break easily, but perhaps fire will melt it."

A cattle herder said to the soldier, "Tethysian, try your dragon!"

The soldier beckoned the talongrunt with a sharp whistle. "Everyone, stand back," he said as the dragon hopped toward them. At the soldier's command, it shot several fireballs at the mound. After the smoke cleared, some held their lanterns up to see if any damage occurred. To their dismay, they found it hadn't softened a bit. It was stone cold to the touch.

"It's cursed," a sailor said. "There's no way we'll be getting Eli out of this."

"What are we going to do?" a young seamstress asked.

"Mommy, I'm scared," Trevor whimpered.

"We'll think of something," the blacksmith said.

A voice familiar to most of those gathered answered from across the plaza, "We'll ask the Great King."

Everyone peered into the darkness, where a single pinprick of lantern-light was approaching.

"Is that...?" the soldier asked, eyes widening.

"No, it can't be!" Caruso breathed.

Sure enough, when the newcomer came close, everyone saw that it was Matthias who had come to join them. He looked shaken and embarrassed to be there, but determined, nonetheless. He repeated, "We'll ask the Great King. He brought us here, and he'll tell us what to do next."

The others agreed, though evidently shocked that it was Matthias, of all people, who suggested it.

"All right. Here goes nothing." The elderly woman cleared her throat. "Great King, what have you brought us here to do?"

The group waited in silence. No one knew what to expect.

A thundering voice?

A messenger pigeon?

A courier on horseback or riding a dragon?

A fairy or nymph?

What if there was no answer at all?

As time went by, the same thought crossed every person's mind, though it was discounted by almost all. It was so simple, so counter-intuitive, given their circumstances. But as the thought persisted, one person dared to suggest it.

"We should sing," Lia said.

No one commented for a few seconds, but Lia persisted, "Mister Eli loved to sing. I think he'll be happy if we sing, too."

"I believe the lass is right," the sailor admitted.

"I had the same thought," the seamstress agreed.

"But what do we sing?" the soldier asked.

Lia replied as if it were obvious. "Eli's *favorite* song!"

"What is it, baby?" Trisha asked.

"It goes…hmm, I think it goes like this:

When there is doubt, I know that hope is best.
When others grieve, a song of joy I'll sing.
When storms abound, in peace, my heart will rest.
I know and trust my father, the King."

"Oh, I remember now!" Trevor said. "Eli sang that all the time. All over the house!"

Caruso chuckled. "Would you kids like to lead us?"

"Sure!" They began singing Eli's favorite song.

Others in the group joined in, quiet at first. It was hard to take the song seriously because no one felt any semblance of hope, joy, or peace. However, as they sang it again and again, their hearts began to warm as they felt those emotions growing within them.

Matthias was the only one who had yet to sing. The thought of singing in general, much less a simple childish tune, grated against his pride. However, Trevor noticed his lack of participation and called him out, "Matthias, the Great King wants to hear your voice, too!"

Matthias nearly choked at the authority in little Trevor's voice, and he started bumbling the words. After singing the song a couple times, he relaxed, as even he became more hopeful, joyful, and peaceful.

The group continued to sing, but aside from the psychological benefits they reaped, nothing in their surroundings changed. Soon, their voices becoming hoarse, they stopped.

In the ensuing silence, they could hear the rustling of the lukú-ba all around them. There was a conversation between two distorted voices:

"They stopped."

"Yes. They realize it's no use."

"The Music of Marindel is not for mortal beings. There's nothing to be concerned about."

"Perhaps so, but clearly they are not frightened enough by our triumph. We must convince them otherwise."

"In time, they will learn. Darkness will rule forever."

"Forever, and ever,"

"And for all time."

The voices cackled, and a distant chorus of laughter echoed all around them.

As the noise faded, Caruso said, "We should go now."

"Where to? What's the point?" the cattle herder asked. "There's no escaping those zombie-monkeys no matter *where* we go. We'll never be safe! You heard 'em!"

"To my manor," Caruso replied. "There's room enough for everyone. We'll last much longer if we stay together, even if this darkness *does* drag on forever."

"Aye," the sailor agreed.

"I'll make sure those monsters don't attack us along the way," Matthias said, placing a hand on his sword hilt. To the soldier, he said, "You and your dragon stay sharp!"

"Yessir!" the soldier replied, hurrying over to his talongrunt.

"I have a sword as well," Auben said to Matthias.

"Good. Keep it ready."

Everyone talked quietly amongst themselves as they left the mound where Eli's body was hidden. As they went, the hope, joy, and peace they just sang about evaporated from their hearts.

Only Lia remained where she was.

She sang Eli's song again, continuing with a few verses she remembered at that moment.

"When there is fear, I'll stand with daring eyes
When others hate, a song of love I'll sing.
When death prevails, in light, I will arise.
I know and trust my father, the King."

"Lia!" Trisha called. "Come on, baby! We're leaving!"

"Coming," Lia answered. With a regretful sigh, she went to join the others. After covering half the distance, she looked back at the mound one last time. When she did, something glittering in the darkness beyond caught her eye.

A small, blue butterfly fluttered toward Point Nex from the sea. To say the butterfly was bioluminescent would be an understatement. It was radiant, sparkling like a star, dancing magnificently in great contrast to its bleak and dreary surroundings.

Lia watched with great intrigue as the butterfly meandered toward the mound and landed at the foot of it, close to where she'd just been standing. She called, "Mommy, look!"

"Lia, come here!" Trisha's back was turned as she endeavored with Auben's help to get up on the horse. "Oh, I can't wait to have this baby already!"

Lia glanced at her mother for a second but then continued to watch the butterfly. It was too beautiful to ignore.

Soon, Lia began to feel tremors in the ground beneath her. To her amazement, small cracks appeared in the mound, quickly spreading and widening. Beams of light pierced through the cracks, intensifying in brightness, and a quiet whirring sound escalated as they spread.

Caruso noticed first and shouted, "Lia! Get away from there!"

Lia obeyed without question. The butterfly also fled, and then the mound shattered from the inside with a brilliant flash of light and a thunderous boom!

Everyone shielded their eyes from the blinding explosion, and several people were knocked down by the shockwave. Fragments of the mound fell upon the group like a hailstorm. But upon contact with them or the ground, the shards disintegrated into black dust and caused no harm.

It took a moment for everyone to become accustomed to the light emanating from the spot the mound once occupied. Soon, they were able to make out the figure of a man standing in the center of the light atop the steps of the altar, the wooden part of which was dismantled behind him. The man was impressive and dazzling, dressed in a stunning white outfit complete with a cape and cavalier. His face was humble and friendly, eyes glimmering, easily recognized by all.

When Caruso rubbed his eyes and looked closer, he lost his breath. "I…I can't believe it! It's…! It's…!"

"Mister Eli!" Trevor and Lia shouted, sprinting toward the altar with joyful shouts.

"It *is* him!" the elderly woman said. "I see him there with my own eyes! He's alive!"

"Eli!" Caruso ran to the altar, followed by almost everyone else.

"Auben!" Trisha yelled after her husband. "Help me off this horse!"

"Oh, right! I'm coming, love!" Auben returned to help his wife off the horse, and they went to the altar together.

As the kids ascended the steps, Eli smiled as big and bright as ever and stooped down to meet them, arms wide. "Trevor! Lia! It's great to see you!"

"You survived!" Trevor shouted, squeezing him tight.

"Not quite, bud. I was dead, but now, by the power of the Great King, I am alive!"

"Wow!" Trevor pulled away from Eli's embrace and ran down the steps toward the others. "Hey, everybody! Eli was dead! But now he's alive!"

Eli chuckled as Trevor ran off, and then to Lia, he said, "You have a wonderful singing voice, my dear. Thank you for listening to the Great King. He and I are very proud of you."

"Thanks," Lia replied, burying her face in his chest.

As everyone gathered around the altar to behold him, the sky began to brighten with the first gleams of dawn. In the midst of this, Eli stood and said, "Hello, my friends! Do not be alarmed. Your eyes do not deceive you. The Great King has breathed new life into my body. He has bestowed upon me the inheritance he has in store for those who follow his will to the very end: the power to triumph over death."

Everyone murmured amongst themselves, hardly able to comprehend Eli's words.

He continued, "I will explain more to you soon. Meet me in the apple orchard outside Diamond City, and there I will speak with you one last time before I return to Marindel. Now, I must finish the work my father started."

Eli looked beyond the group, where hundreds of lukúba were gathered. They'd been creeping out of hiding ever since the mound shattered, but no one noticed until Eli turned his attention to them. They were gawking and pointing, squabbling and shrieking, unable to look at Eli but evidently confused as to why he wasn't dead.

Eli leapt with a front flip, soaring over his friends, and landed amid the lukúba. He looked at them with a smirk, bold and unafraid. "What's the matter? Surprised?"

They screamed and shielded their eyes, scrambling backward to distance themselves from him.

Eli sang a verse, his pure Elvish words dripping with magical strength, and a sword of light formed in his right hand. With blinding speed, he turned on the nearest three lukúba and sliced them in half. They slumped to the ground, turned pasty-gray, and disintegrated like windblown ashes.

They were most certainly dead.

Seeing this, the lukúba in the plaza dispersed at once. Many more jettisoned from the crags and trees surrounding Point Nex, and they all fled in retreat.

"You won't get far!" Eli called, flipping his sword in his hand and beginning to run toward the exit of Point Nex. He cleared the plaza in a few seconds before jumping onto the crags, where he jumped from rock to rock and from tree to tree. He was faster than the lukúba, even as they flew helter-skelter in panic. Whenever he caught up to one, he killed it.

The unicorn, watching all of this, whinnied with delight and galloped after Eli. Its mystical powers enabled it to run faster than any ordinary horse.

Eli's friends watched with awe, rendered breathless and unable to say a word.

Once he reached level ground beyond the mountains, Eli ran through the woods. His focus was unbreakable, and the zealous fire in his eyes, unquenchable. Nothing could deter him from his mission, the beauty he sought to rescue.

As he broke out of the woods and raced across the grassland, the unicorn caught up and ran alongside him. Seeing it, Eli jumped onto its back and began to sing. Tendrils of light enveloped the sprinting unicorn and caused it to grow larger and more radiant. Magnificent, feathered wings sprouted on the unicorn's body, and at the conclusion of Eli's song, the magical steed launched into the sky with incredible speed and a jubilant whinny.

The Serpent's minions across the land were flushed out of the shadows and forced to flee by the brilliant light of Eli's presence. Singing once more, Eli crafted his sword into a bow and sent arrows of light after the fleeing lukúba. The projectiles speared multiple creatures at once. Many of them perished in their haste to escape the risen Prince.

En masse, squealing for their lives, the lukúba fled toward Diamond City.

"Put me down!" The Tethysian governor writhed and dangled by the nape of his tunic, which was secured in the jaws of the Serpent. "Help! Somebody help!"

The Serpent purred with delight, reveling in the terrified screams of the governor as he shook him back and forth. He tossed the governor high in the air and said, "You're not having as much fun as I thought you would. Does this game bore you? Don't worry, I have a better idea for you, just like I did for your white-bearded friend. I can feel my belly rumble as he fights to escape. Come and join him!" The Serpent opened his mouth wide, ready to catch the governor and swallow him whole.

A shriek caught the Serpent's attention, and he looked for the source. The governor landed on the Serpent's head, tumbling down the length of his neck before falling and landing in a sticky pile of sludge.

At that time, Diamond City was in the midst of a slow and dreadful destruction. The palace was a wreck, covered in sludge and crushed beneath the weight of the Serpent, who coiled comfortably upon its ruins. The lukúba had caused widespread devastation across the rest of the city. However, such things were only visible now that the sky glowed pink and blue with the coming of sunrise.

The shriek that distracted the Serpent also caught the attention of his minions. Hearing the distant squeals of their brethren in panic, they, too, began to screech and take flight. Giving no heed to the Great Serpent's will, the lukúba scattered in frenzied haste to escape the return of the light.

So great was their fear of Eli.

As the lukúba dispersed, the Serpent squinted to see what all the commotion was about. Beyond the incoming swarms of terrified creatures, backed by the rising sun as it peeked over the horizon, the Serpent saw the brightest light he had ever seen—and in the midst of it all, a man on a winged horse.

The Serpent immediately knew who it was. He blinked hard, gaping in unbelief. "What? No! *Impossible!*"

As lukúba zipped past him, the Serpent heard them screaming the name of Eli in sheer panic. He roared at his minions, unable to contain the fear in his voice, "Where do you think you're going!? Come back here! Hold together!"

The lukúba ignored him.

The Serpent looked at Eli once more, eyes wide. The Great Prince was approaching fast, his vengeful gaze locked on the Serpent.

"Agh! This cannot be!" The Serpent yowled, maneuvering his enormous coiling body out of the palace ruins and beginning to fly upward in a tight spiral.

Eli watched as the Serpent flew higher and higher. He pat the neck of his steed and said, "We're not letting him get away. After him!"

The winged unicorn veered upward, its wings and hooves pounding the air in pursuit.

The Serpent flew so high that the entire island of Rhema was visible from his altitude. When he saw Eli hot on his trail, he turned to face him. The Serpent flexed his body, flaring every one of his fins, flukes, spines, and tendrils. The thin yellow markings on his body radiated with magical power. The Serpent opened his mouth wide, allowing an orb of iridescent energy to form within, and he launched the orb at his pursuer with supersonic speed.

Eli sang once again.

The Serpent's attack shattered on an invisible barrier in front of Eli and the unicorn. The impact of sparks and smoke hid them for a moment, but they shot out of the fray undeterred.

"No!" The Serpent curled his lips, bared his teeth, and roared. "Who do you think you are, Great Prince!? How *dare* you defy the laws of death and challenge me!"

Without slowing his approach, Eli said, "I am the son of the Great King, whom you have defied from the very beginning. You've taken something precious from me, and I'm going to take it back!"

"You can't! I claimed this power and authority fair and square! You know it's true! Only the girl can take it back, and you and I know she *never* will!"

"I took her place, remember? Now it's mine to reclaim." Eli smirked, drawing his bow. "Besides, I wasn't talking about *that*."

The Serpent had no time to react before Eli planted a light arrow in his face. The bolt's impact ripped off one of the Serpent's neck spines, and he yowled in pain.

As the winged horse passed over the Serpent, Eli jumped and dove straight into his mouth.

His yowl ending in a muddled choke, the Serpent tried to clear his throat and unwittingly began hacking like a cat with a hairball. After several seconds of this, the Serpent's face contorted. Tears of pain welled up in the corners of his eyes. His entire body convulsed, and he vomited, spewing a mixture of blood and black dust along with Eli and his own severed tongue.

While in free-fall, Eli used his sword of light to cut into the Serpent's tongue, and he extracted an unconscious Melody from its fleshy bowels. Once he had an arm wrapped securely around her, he transformed his sword into a lasso, which he tossed at his incoming winged horse. When the lasso snagged around the horse's neck, the rope retracted to pull Eli and Melody up onto its back.

In denial, despite his great pain, the Serpent howled and dove after them.

Down they went, falling toward Diamond City, sprawled beneath them. As they plummeted, Eli used the lasso to secure Melody to the horse's back. Then he said, "Take her safely to the ground. I'll be back."

Eli jumped backward off the horse and allowed himself to be swallowed by the Serpent, this time going well past the throat.

Almost at the ground, the winged horse slowed its descent and alighted on the wall of the city. Then it turned to face the Serpent.

Realizing he had eaten Eli, the Serpent sneered and slowed his descent as well. Taking a position facing the winged horse, he tried to speak but only gurgled and spewed bloodied black dust from his mouth. Growling angrily, he spoke telepathically instead. *The poor Prince put up a grand fight, but he will not survive. Seven thousand times more potent than the saliva of Nex, surely my stomach acid will devour him and his hideous, glowing glory within moments.* He lowered his head, furrowed his brow, and bared his blood-stained teeth in a snarl. *Put the girl down NOW! I'm taking her back, and no one will see her ever again. She is mine! She will ALWAYS be mine!*

The horse stood its ground with a snort, brandishing its horn and flaring its wings.

The Serpent roared, rearing up in preparation to strike. At the moment of climax, just before he crashed down upon them, the Serpent's belly was split clean open by a ray of light. The fissure spread like a jagged lightning bolt all the way up to his throat. The Serpent's eyes widened just before his head exploded. What remained of his hovering body disintegrated into black dust and was dispersed by a strong wind.

From the blast that impacted the Serpent's head came Eli, flipping through the air, sword in hand. After landing beside his steed, he reached up and caught another object flying from the explosion. He opened his palm to admire the item.

Melody's amulet. Her inheritance from the Great King.

He tucked it away in his pocket, dismissed his sword, and looked up with a grand smile and arms stretched upward. "Father, I've done it!"

"Well done, my son," the Great King answered, his voice resounding across the blue sky. "However, this is far from over. It is only the beginning."

Comprehension

1) On his way to Point Nex, Caruso senses that a greater power is at work, like he did during Eli's trial. What's different about this time?

2) Which notable characters meet Caruso at Point Nex? Why are they all there?

3) What creature appears after the group sings Eli's Song? What does it symbolize?

4) What is the most prominent feature of Eli's fighting style?

5) Why does Eli now have the authority to directly challenge the Serpent?

6) How does Eli rescue Melody? What does this symbolize?

7) What object does Eli claim from the Serpent?

Reflection

1)Describe a time when you or a loved one received a breakthrough in a difficult situation because you chose a posture of worship (you can use the same situation from your last chapter's reflection, if applicable). Can you think of any stories in Scripture when God's people used worship as warfare?

14

The Prince of Victory
Summer, 104 IE

The people of Diamond City soon realized the danger was gone, and they came out of their hiding places. Hardly anyone saw Eli battling the Serpent, and those who did were unable to recognize him. Even so, they celebrated, relieved that the monsters were gone and the daylight had returned. By then, Eli and the winged horse had already left the city.

At noon on the same day, Eli's friends arrived at the apple orchard. Everyone was on horseback except for the soldier, who rode his talongrunt. Matthias was reunited with his thunderbeast shortly after the lukúba fled. They found Eli reclining against a tree trunk, munching on an apple. The winged horse grazed nearby, and Melody lay asleep in a soft bed of green grass. Everyone dismounted and gathered around him, still hardly able to express their awe. Eli rose to greet them, hugging and shaking hands and smiling like he always did. Together, they celebrated the events of the day.

Matthias was the sole exception. He was filled with remorse for the role he played in Eli's arrest and death, so he stood at a distance. He didn't believe Eli would want to see him because of what he did.

Soon, Eli looked at him and asked, "Matthias, what troubles you?"

Breathing hard, trying in vain to hide his fear, Matthias walked up to Eli and got down on one knee. He looked him in the eye and said, "Prince Eli, I...I'm *so* sorry...for everything."

Eli smiled and extended his hand.

After a moment's hesitation, Matthias took Eli's hand and allowed himself to be pulled up. He was caught off guard when Eli embraced him. Slowly, he returned the embrace and began to weep. Then Eli took him by the shoulders and said, "I forgive you, friend."

The others cheered, coming to pat Matthias on the back and continue celebrating. They enjoyed apples from the tree in abundance, since they hadn't eaten for the duration of the Serpent's attack on Rhema.

"You did it, didn't you?" the seamstress asked Eli as they ate. "You killed the Great Serpent!"

"Not quite. I destroyed his physical form and robbed him of his power. But his spirit still lives. He will continue in his devious ways to gain back his strength and defy the Kingdom of Marindel until the very last day." He took out Melody's amulet and held it up for all to see. "The Great King would like for you to carry this authority in your hearts as you live your lives, day by day, listening to his voice and caring for others just like you saw me do. Follow in my footsteps and teach others to do the same. As you do, you will prepare the way for the return of the Kingdom of Marindel."

Eli clasped his hands over the amulet and rubbed them together. He opened his hands to breathe deeply upon it, and then he tossed it up as if releasing a dove. The amulet soared like a shooting star before exploding into millions of magical sparks, which dispersed as far as the eye could see on every horizon. Some of the sparks lingered and were absorbed into every person present.

As they beheld the wondrous spectacle, Eli declared, "Now, *all* who declare allegiance to the Great King will be adopted into his family as sons and daughters of royalty! Those who choose to receive their inheritance will be victorious in this realm and in the Kingdom of Marindel when it returns. But always remember: just as the Serpent deceived Melody into surrendering her inheritance, so the Serpent will try to deceive every one of you. Be vigilant and resist him at every opportunity, looking out for one another and covering each other's weaknesses. As children of the Great King, you're more powerful than that foul beast, but he will try to blind you to that truth. Never forget who you are. And never forget my love for you, nor the love of our father, the Great King."

"How long will you stay with us?" Trisha asked.

"The time has come for me to return to Marindel. Though I'll be gone for a while, you must begin undoing the works of the Serpent by loving others, standing up for the innocent, and telling all sentient creatures about the Great King so they may come to know him."

Eli turned and walked toward Melody, his beloved. He knelt close to her and whispered, "I love you, Mel. I will always love you, and I promise I will return for you when you call for me." He kissed her forehead.

Melody breathed deeply, though she didn't wake up.

Eli stood and addressed the others, "Take good care of her in my absence. The Serpent will continue to deceive her, and she will continue to be stubborn, but the seeds of renewal have been planted in her heart. Nurture them well by proving the Great King's love for her until the final day. I promise. I will return!"

After he finished speaking, Eli went out to the field and mounted his horse. Caruso followed him and asked, "Will we ever see you again?"

"Yes, but not here."

Caruso looked away sadly. "You're the best thing that's ever happened to Rhema. We will all miss you."

"Cheer up!" Eli said with a twinkle in his eye. "I cannot stay, but I'll tell you who can: two friends of yours who gave their lives resisting the Serpent and his dark forces."

Caruso looked at Eli with a raised eyebrow.

Eli smiled. "I know how much they meant to you. Consider it a parting gift."

The yowl of a dracoviper prompted Caruso to turn around. Sure enough, Hunter and Kaya were flying toward him, chirping and yowling with glee.

"Ah! Hunter! Kaya!" Caruso shouted, running to meet his dragons as they landed in the grass and tackled him. "Oh, I'm so glad you're all right! I thought I would never see you again!"

Eli laughed, and then he said to the others gathered, "I bid you farewell, and I look forward to the day we'll meet again. Always remember, though you will not see me, I will always be with you. And I will always love you, my friends, and fellow heirs to the throne of Marindel!"

Without further ado, Eli urged the winged horse to fly, and with a triumphant whinny, it launched into the sky.

As the others watched him go, Matthias ran toward his thunderbeast and said, "Let's go see him off!"

"I'm in!" the pineapple farmer said, running after Matthias.

"And I!" the sailor followed the pineapple farmer.

"Me, too!" Trevor shouted.

"You're too small to ride a dragon," Auben said with a laugh.

"You and the kids can ride Kaya," Caruso said.

Auben turned serious, clearly not fond of the idea, but Trevor and Lia's excited whoops convinced him. He looked at Trisha for approval, and she said with a chuckle, "Just this once."

As Eli soared higher and higher, many of Eli's friends followed him: Matthias, the pineapple farmer, and the sailor aboard the thunderbeast; the Tethysian soldier aboard his talongrunt; Caruso aboard Hunter; and Auben, Trevor, and Lia aboard Kaya. Everyone else watched from below, looking up at Eli's departing figure until he vanished from sight.

Those flying after Eli last saw him disappear between two cumulus clouds. As they went through the clouds after him, all they saw in the blue sky beyond were glimmers of fading magic. They heard Eli's voice echo on the wind, "Remember, I will always love you, my friends and fellow heirs to the throne of Marindel!"

Comprehension

1) Why is Matthias hesitant to approach Eli? How does Eli respond?

2) What does Eli do to Melody's amulet? What does it symbolize?

3) List three commands Eli gives to his friends.

4) When will Eli return?

Reflection

1) Think about the moment you received Jesus as your Savior. Imagine Him appearing there, smiling brilliantly, and giving you an amulet that carries the same authority, power, and access to the Father that He has. Do you see yourself carrying this authority in your daily life? Why or why not?

Epilogue
The Final Days
Winter, 198 IE

L ia the Seer, princess of Marindel and daughter of the Great King,

To Prince Vitaly of the Northern Wilds, my son in allegiance to the Great King,

May the strength and favor of Prince Eli's gaze invigorate your spirit.

Since our last encounter, my heart has burned with radiant joy because of the incredible calling the Great King has bestowed upon you. Please don't take it for granted, as the Serpent will tempt you to do. It's no simple matter to deliver the kingdoms of the realm from the most catastrophic era of tyranny we have ever known.

For two hundred years, the Tethysian Empire has pillaged and conquered all sentient life. They have especially scorned our family, the citizens of the Kingdom of Marindel. The Empire's irreverent arrogance and the fervent cries of the oppressed have filled the Great King's heart with anguish, and soon, he'll do away with them once and for all. Our

King is kind and compassionate, patient and forgiving—but woe to the kingdom that provokes his rage!

Their end is coming soon: a day of darkness and gloom, of fire and steel. The wings of their dragons will blot out the sun, and their roars will shake the earth as they make their defiance known. But like their master, whom they blindly follow, their destruction has already been decreed. The Tethysian Empire will shatter like pottery, and the liberated provinces will prosper. In years to come, no one will remember the strength and splendor of Tethys, nor will they trade with them because Tethys will cease to be a kingdom.

You, dear prince, will see this day, according to the commission given to you by the Great Prince of the Sea. Even now, I advise you to begin mobilizing the mainland peoples. Encourage them with stories of Marindel, and teach them to act justly and fight with courage. And you must diligently hone the gifts of fire and lightning given to you on the mountain. Your abilities will grow stronger if you do so in the presence of the Music of Marindel, and they may even become infused with light.

Do not be disheartened or impatient regarding the timing of these things. Though it may seem far off now, always remain vigilant. You will know the hour of the Empire's end, and I trust that you will be ready.

But that isn't the reason I've written. What I have to share with you now concerns the final days and the return of the Kingdom of Marindel.

From the Era of Peace until now, the Great King has sought after Melody, whom he loves fiercely with all his heart. He has raised up many Seers and gifted individuals—warriors, musicians, politicians, and masters of all trades—to remind her of Prince Eli's love. But to this day, she hasn't listened. Since Rhema was destroyed and her crown was revoked, she has become difficult to locate. The Great Prince warned us that she would continue in her stubbornness, and if I hadn't any discernment—if I didn't know the Great King's plan for redemption—I'd say she's worse off now than before. Only by remembering Eli's love for us, and also for her, are we able to continue pursuing her. These are the troubles we're facing all across the realm pertaining to the former queen of Rhema.

However, a time will come when Melody will remember everything, unhindered by the lies of the Serpent, as Prince Eli declared. The Great King's appointed herald, through courageous love and determination, will draw her gently into the camp of the Great King. The island of Rhema, though long forsaken, will once again take its place among the kingdoms of the realm. This sign will be a shining beacon of hope to all who declare allegiance to the Great King of Marindel.

At the same time, the realm will be deceived by the Great Serpent. He will appear to them as Eli did to us—as a man, charming and wise—and he will appoint himself the "great king" of a Rebellious Empire. Boasting of their knowledge, drunk with power, and united as one, they will reject the ways of the Great King and attempt to destroy Melody once and for all. The might of their forces will greatly exceed that of the Tethysian Empire, and all who behold them will be sick with terror. Nothing like this has ever happened before, nor will it ever happen again.

But even then, out of every kingdom, a remnant will remain steadfast to resist the will of the Serpent, and they will assemble as one to defend Melody in her darkest hour. The Rebellious Empire will hunt them down with ravenous loathing, and many servants of the King will be lost. However, the Great King himself will declare war on the Rebellious Empire. Great will be their misery—for he will inflict upon them tremendous judgments far worse than anything they could ever throw at Melody and the citizens of Marindel. But they will not relent or turn from their hatred. With hearts of stone, they'll continue in rebellion to the very end.

In the midst of this, at long last, Melody will claim her authority as the beloved bride of the Great Prince and the apple of her father's eye. Only then will she call for the Great Prince of the Sea. And only then will he return, as a mighty warrior, to avenge himself on the Great Serpent and the Rebellious Empire which sought the blood of his beloved. Only then, after their permanent destruction by the sword of his song, will there be everlasting peace in the realm of Tyrizah.

As the Great King once said, "There will come a day when humans, elves, and sentient creatures from every kingdom will live in Marindel side-by-side." Those who've fallen, together with those still living, will rise again at the moment Prince Eli appears. Death will be abolished, and a new era of peace will endure forever under the perfect reign of the Great Prince and his beloved!

Who is wise like the Great King of the Sea? Who can challenge truth and expect to win? The kingdoms rise; they band together and plot for conquest. They assemble on the day of battle to crush the children of the light. But the Great King is in their midst! To the dismay of his enemies, the King declares, "I have given the kingdoms of Tyrizah to my son, the Great Prince. Who can take from him what his father, the King, has given? Surely he will rule forever and ever!"

Prince Eli's leadership is of the highest quality. He excels in every way!

He is devoted to his father, the King, and to Melody, his beloved, with vigorous zeal.

His wisdom is the very wisdom of the Great King.

His emotions, passions, and affections are extravagant in their abundance and diversity.

His words are sweet and pure, enlightening and convicting, alive and creative, always giving life to those who bear his name—and terror to those who stand opposed.

His ways and purposes unfold with strength, orderliness, beauty, and permanence.

His impartation of royal authority upon all sentient beings is a tremendous honor and a wonderful mystery.

Friendship with him is sweetness itself. Nothing is more delightful!

His tender compassion is wholesome and dynamic, with the power to heal every heart.

He is radiant in his majesty, beautiful in his love, and he humbled himself to be our friend.

Remember him now, though he may seem far off. Remember his love, because one day, he will return—and great will be his throne!

Vitaly, dear one, you know how crafty the Serpent can be. Treasure these words in your heart, and they will keep your hope alive when the days of darkness come. For us, this concerns the end of the Imperial Era. For generations yet to come, this concerns the end of the Great Serpent.

Write a copy of this manuscript and send it to the scribes at Besaadin, in the province of Sunophsis. They're diligently working to preserve the stories of Marindel, not the least of which includes the Great Story and most of the letters we've written from Rhema's destruction until now. Take every precaution to ensure this letter never falls into Imperial hands.

May you continue to grow in favor and standing with all people, and may the wisdom of the Great King guide your decisions. Lastly, always remember the Great Prince Eli's love for you.

Comprehension

1) How much time has passed since the events of the last chapter?

2) Why do you think, after everything Eli did, Lia suggests Melody may be worse off than before?

3) List two similarities and two differences between the Tethysian Empire and the Rebellious Empire.

4) What will be the final destiny of the Great Serpent and the Rebellious Empire?

5) List five attributes of the Great Prince Eli.

Reflection

1) Describe how Jesus meets you personally in each of the five ways you listed above. If you're unsure, write a prayer asking Jesus to reveal Himself to you in those ways.

Further Reflection and Biblical Integration

Now that you've finished reading the Great Story, challenge yourself by reflecting on themes and symbols of the allegory in relation to the truth of God's Word. Answer the following questions on a separate sheet of paper or in your journal, and/or discuss them in your group.

1) In your own words, summarize the Great King's plan to rescue Melody and overcome the Great Serpent. Compare and contrast it with God's plan for salvation, including relevant Scripture.

2) Reflect on the character of the Great King as an allegory for Father God. In your own words, describe how Father God relates to us as His adopted children. Can you support your answer with Scripture?

3) Reflect on the character of Prince Eli as an allegory for Jesus Christ. In your own words, describe the personality of Jesus as 1) the visible representation of the Father, 2) the Bridegroom, and 3) the Victorious King. Can you support your answer with Scripture?

4) Recall Eli's words, "The forces of darkness have come to eclipse the light, but soon the light will return." Define the words "Penumbra," "Umbra," and "Antumbra," and describe how a solar eclipse might symbolize Jesus' death and resurrection.

5) Reflect on the character of Melody as an allegory for the people of Israel. In your own words, describe the role of Israel as God's chosen people. Can you support your answer with Scripture?

6) Read Romans 11. What will be the final destiny of Israel? Why do you think it's important for Gentile believers to understand this? Can you support your answer with Scripture?

7) Reflect on "all sentient beings" as an allegory for the Gentiles—people from every tribe, tongue, and nation. In your own words, describe their role in God's story of redemption, contrasting with that of Israel. Can you support your answer with Scripture?

8) Reflect on the character of the Great Serpent as an allegory for Satan. In your own words, describe the cunning tactics of the devil to destroy God's people. After Jesus' death and resurrection, what power does he have over us? How might we respond to his devious attacks? Can you support your answer with Scripture?

9) Reflect on the prominence of song, or spoken word, in the Great Story. In your own words, describe how it illustrates the creative power of God's Word and the power of the tongue. Can you support your answer with Scripture?

10) Eschatology—the study of the end times—is a subject of much debate amongst honest, Bible-believing scholars. Nevertheless, it's undeniably a theme of great importance in Scripture, and for us, as we near the final days of our current era. Have you taken the time to study eschatology for yourself? Why or why not? Write down where you will start or how you will add to your learning.

Creative Ideas for Immersive Reflection

Explore the characters and themes of *The Great Story of Marindel* with a creative project. Below are a few ideas for inspiration. Have fun!

1) Draw a comic strip of at least four panels depicting your favorite scene from the Great Story.

2) Imagine yourself in the place of Melody, and Jesus in the place of Eli. Write a conversational-style poem or letter expressing your feelings and concerns to Jesus, followed by His response to you. Go back and forth at least twice.

3) On a poster or piece of cardboard, cut and paste a collage of words and images that remind you of the most impacting moments of the Great Story.

4) Compose music on your instrument of choice to accompany the words of Eli's Song. Record yourself playing (and singing, if possible) the song.

5) With friends or family, act out your favorite scene from the Great Story. Get as creative as you'd like with props and costumes. Record yourselves performing the skit.

6) Create an animated short film depicting your favorite scene from the Great Story.

Acknowledgments

First of all, thank you to the faculty of Western Christian High School, where I was invited to speak about my author's journey and the inspiration behind *The Epic of Marindel: Chosen*. That experience is what opened my mind to the idea of creating a study book based on the Great Story.

To my beta readers, Greg, Jonathon, Neil, and Sarah, and to my editor, Melodie Fox, thank you for providing valuable insight, encouragement, and instruction on how to structure this book. Your feedback was priceless as I delved into this new genre of writing.

To the COVID-19 pandemic, however ironic, thank you for redirecting my life in such a way that gave me the opportunity to prepare this book for such a time as this. You will be over soon, and no one will miss you.

Finally, my highest thanks and praises go to my Lord Jesus Christ, the Great Prince, for whom and about whom this story has been written. Thank You for inviting me to write this inspiring, unique, and timely epic fantasy series about Your pursuit of Your Beloved. This year has not been easy, but You have sustained me through it all. You are worthy. May You be glorified, above all else, by the impact of *The Great Story of Marindel*.

The Adventure Continues in The Epic of Marindel: Chosen!

Over 1500 years have passed since Eli defeated the Great Serpent in Rhema. The Tethysian Empire has long since fallen, and new kingdoms have risen to take its place. Nearly every memory of the Great King, Prince Eli, and Melody has been erased from history. The Kingdom of Marindel has been reduced to a mere folk tale one might hear from a shady traveler in a tavern on a stormy night.

But the final days are nigh. The Great King's appointed herald must rise and unite a new generation of heroes against the Great Serpent's final campaign of rebellion. But first, he must realize he's more than just a simple farmer with a wild imagination. It may take a surprise encounter with Melody to get him on the right track—but will he be able to stand against the dark forces pursuing her at every turn?

Embark on the adventure of a lifetime in Book I of the award-winning fantasy series, *The Epic of Marindel: Chosen*! Order it online from Amazon or any bookstore or retail website.

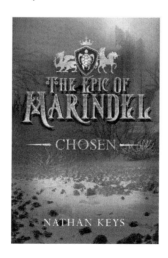

Guest Speaker

Nathan Keys

www.nathankeys.com

Award-Winning Author and Speaker

Nathan's vocation is to write empowering stories that captivate readers and leave them with hope and purpose. His passion is to help others pursue their creative calling by equipping them to understand their identity in Christ and overcome obstacles of discouragement, unworthiness, and lack of vision.

He believes that every person has a story, and every story is a part of something Greater.

Topics:
- Literary and Biblical influences behind Marindel
- World-building and character development in fiction
- How to establish a writing routine
- Owning your identity in Christ
- Discovering God's delight in you
- Discerning and pursuing your God-given calling

Great for:
- Conferences
- Reading/Writing Groups
- Bible Studies
- Men's Groups
- Classroom Guest Speaker

Book to Speak: epicofmarindel@nathankeys.com

Made in the USA
Las Vegas, NV
23 February 2021

18441345R00136